His gaze lingered on her mouth. "I've been thinking a lot lately about your advice."

"What advice?"

"You know what you always say about going after what you want? Like when a guy wants something very badly, but the risks are damned high?"

"I guess that would depend on how much you're willing to lose," she answered very softly.

He searched her face. And then he sighed lightly, dropped his hand and moved an inch backward. "Some things are just too valuable to gamble on."

She reached out and caught his shirt. Giving a little tug, she brought him back to within touching proximity. "Some risks are worth taking."

Dear Reader,

As she starts her third year of medical training, halfway to graduation, Haley Wright hopes she'll be assigned to rotations with her best friend, Anne Easton. Instead, she finds herself sharing those assignments with another member of her close-knit, five-member study group—Ron Gibson. Haley considers Ron a friend, but it's no secret that the two of them have had a sometimes volatile relationship. For two years, they've set off sparks when they're together, and Haley has always attributed those fireworks to Ron's ability to set off her rare temper with his relentless teasing. But lately she's beginning to wonder if it's a different kind of heat flaring between them....

I've had so much fun writing the Doctors in Training series and "matching up" the members of the study group I introduced in *Diagnosis: Daddy.* I hope you've enjoyed the stories, too, and that you'll attend their graduation from medical school in the next book, James Stillman's story, *Prognosis: Romance.*

Visit me at ginawilkins.com.

Gina Wilkins

THE DOCTOR'S UNDOING

GINA WILKINS

SPECIAL EDITION®

Published by Silhouette Books

America's Publisher of Contemporary Romance

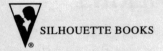 SILHOUETTE BOOKS

ISBN-13: 978-0-373-65539-7

Recycling programs
for this product may
not exist in your area.

THE DOCTOR'S UNDOING

Visit Silhouette Books at www.eHarlequin.com

Printed in U.S.A.

Books by Gina Wilkins

GINA WILKINS

is a bestselling and award-winning author who has written more than seventy novels for Harlequin and Silhouette Books. She credits her successful career in romance to her long, happy marriage and her three "extraordinary" children.

A lifelong resident of central Arkansas, Ms. Wilkins sold her first book to Harlequin in 1987 and has been writing full-time since. She has appeared on the Waldenbooks, B. Dalton and *USA TODAY* bestseller lists. She is a three-time recipient of the Maggie Award for Excellence, sponsored by Georgia Romance Writers, and has won several awards from the reviewers of *RT Book Reviews*.

For the Insomniac Divas, my light in the darkness.
And with thanks, as always, to Kerry
for her invaluable assistance!

Chapter One

"Will you marry me?"

Haley Wright smiled fondly at the man who had just popped the question—for the third time that week. "It's sweet of you to ask, but I'm afraid I can't."

He sighed heavily. "Already married, huh?"

He responded that same way every time she turned him down. "No, still single." It was the same reply she always gave him. "Just too busy to get married right now."

"I could make things easier for you," he suggested hopefully. "I'm a great cook. I can even do the laundry."

"As much as I appreciate the offer," she said, making a note on the pad in her hand, "I still have to decline."

Edgar Eddington, a sixty-two-year-old Caucasian male presenting with congestive heart failure and cirrhosis of the liver, nodded in resignation against the pillow of the hospital bed in which he lay. "Can't blame a guy for asking a pretty young doctor."

Smiling, Haley looked over her notes to make sure she had everything she needed when she presented her patient to the other students, the residents and the attending physician when they made rounds a short time later. Assuring herself that she had checked everything she was supposed to know about Mr. Eddington for that morning—she hoped—she held her notebook at her side and smiled at the patient. "I'll see you in a little while, Mr. Eddington."

He winked, a flirtatious smile lighting his illness-ravaged face. "I'll look forward to it, doctor."

She had told him several times that as a third-year medical student, she wasn't yet entitled to be called *doctor,* but his answer to that was always, "Close enough." Many patients on her internal medicine rotation tended to call anyone in a white coat "doctor," making no distinction between the students' shorter, hip-length white coats and the physicians' longer coats, which fell almost to the knees. While she had been instructed to politely correct the misidentification, she was not expected to argue with the more stubborn patients.

Hurrying toward the students' room in hopes of snagging a free computer on which to write her notes, she was still smiling a little in response to Mr. Eddington's outrageous flirting. She never failed to be impressed by his bravely cheerful attitude even in the face of the pain he suffered in what both he and the medical staff realized was the final stage of his life. He had weeks to live, at the most, but during the days she had worked with him, she had never once heard him complain.

She was assigned to monitor three patients during the month she would spend on wards in the Veterans Administration hospital near her medical school campus. When one patient was discharged, she picked up another, so she always had three.

Every morning at six, she visited each patient to record any problems noted during the night, to make note of the vital signs that had been taken every two to four hours and to ask if they had any questions or concerns. She always did a physical exam—checking head, eyes, ears, nose, throat, heart, lungs, abdomen, blood flow, pulses in the hands and feet—writing down what she observed. Because she'd been doing those exams for only a week during this, her first rotation, she tried to look more confident than she actually felt.

After she had seen her assigned patients, she had to write notes on each before rounds started at 8:00 a.m. It wasn't easy getting it all done in time, but she knew better than to be late or unprepared when her resident or attending physician asked her a question during rounds.

Aware of rapidly passing minutes, she rushed into the students' room, hoping a computer there would be free. If not, she would have to find an available one somewhere on the floor, and she had very little time remaining before rounds. To her relief, only one of the two computers was being used. Sandy-haired Ron Gibson looked up from the keyboard with a grin when she stumbled into the room. "Running late again?"

She glared at him. "That's easy for you to say. You only had two patients to see today. I had three."

"Maybe if you didn't spend so much time flirting with Mr. Eddington…"

Plopping into the uncomfortable chair in front of the spare computer, she snorted. "Says the guy who can usually be found flirting with the nurses."

"What can I say? They love me."

Sadly enough, it was true. Ron was most definitely the nurses' pet student. His infectious grin and twinkling blue eyes helped him get away with things no other student would even attempt. He was also a favorite with his patients, treating them with respect and sincere concern.

Haley had always known Ron would be a good doctor, even though his sometimes lackadaisical attitude toward class work and studying had frustrated her. They'd both been active in a five-member study group which had drifted together their first semester of medical school and had met frequently afterward, becoming close friends during the first two years of classes. Still, spending so much time together had inevitably led to occasional tension. Haley was aware that she and Ron had contributed perhaps more than their share toward that friction.

It was just that he was so skilled at pushing her buttons, she thought as her fingers flew over the computer keyboard. He liked to tease her about being the perky "cheerleader" of the group, a moniker he used whenever she tried to convince him to take their studies more seriously. It frustrated her that his stated motto had always been, "If it doesn't work out, walk away." Her own had always been, "If at first you don't succeed, keep at it until you do."

Those opposing viewpoints had led more than once to nervous sniping. Fortunately, they had cleared the air between them a couple months ago, and they'd been getting along much better since. She could say honestly that she considered him one of her closest friends.

Pulling her notebook out of one of the stuffed pockets of her pristine white coat, she concentrated on typing her notes. SOAP notes, they were called. *S* for subjective, or what the patient said about his condition overnight. *O* for objective, which included readings of vital signs, lab work and physical exams. *A* for assessment, a brief statement of the patients' descriptions and conditions. And *P* for plan, the recommended course of treatment as prescribed by the resident physician.

A wadded sheet of paper hit her in the back of the head and tumbled to the floor. She didn't even look around. "Stop it, Ron. I'm running out of time."

He laughed softly. Despite her irritation with him, her lips twitched in a wannabe smile. It was a common response to his—okay, she would admit it—his sexy, low laugh. Acknowledging his appeal didn't mean she was particularly susceptible to it, she assured herself, as she had on more than one occasion during the past two years. Ron Gibson was a walking heartbreak if she'd ever met one, and she was too smart and too busy to let herself fall into that trap.

"You know you'll be ready for rounds," he said as he gathered his own notes to stuff into the pocket of his slightly crumpled white coat. "You're a resident's dream of a med student."

It was the student's job to make the resident look good in front of the attending, and Haley acknowledged that she always tried her best to do so. That was her nature—Ron could call it "cheerleader" if he liked, but it was important to her to see others succeed, just as it was for her to do well, herself.

"I try."

"Yes, you certainly do."

Was that a dig? She shot a suspicious look over her shoulder, but couldn't tell anything from his bland demeanor. "It would be better for you if you didn't always have to be the class clown. Your resident spends the whole time during rounds worrying about what you're going to say in front of the attending."

His expression turned instantly innocent. "I've been perfectly well behaved during my presentations."

"Mmm. Doesn't prevent everyone from worrying about when you're going to stop being perfectly well behaved and let your real self show," she muttered, returning to her notes.

He laughed again as he ambled out of the room. "See you on rounds."

Even as she concentrated on finishing her work, she dwelled on thoughts of Ron during the next few minutes. She found it ironic that out of their entire study group, she and Ron were the only two who'd ended up on the same rotation, so they saw each other every day during rounds and lectures.

She'd hoped to share the experience with her best friend, Anne Easton. But Anne was on surgical rotation—a demanding, time-consuming block—in addition to starting a new life with her husband, who now made his home with his wife here in Little Rock when he wasn't traveling for his job. Haley and Anne hardly had a chance to see each other lately. Nor had Haley seen much of Connor or James, their other two study partners. Connor and James were on a separate semester schedule, meaning she wouldn't do any of her rotations with them this year.

She couldn't say she missed the mind-numbing overload of lectures and exams that had taken up the first two years of medical school, but she did miss her friends. Which, perhaps, explained why she was always happy to see Ron every morning, despite her frequent annoyance with him.

Funny how conflicted her feelings were about Ron, she mused, folding her notes into the patient history and physicals—commonly referred to as H & Ps—and slipping them into her pocket. Anne had once commented that Haley and Ron were like squabbling siblings—and yet that description had never felt quite right to Haley. She refused to concede that the sparks she and Ron set off were at all sexual—but "sisterly" wasn't the word she'd have chosen, either. She'd settled for thinking of him as an attractive, interesting, complicated and often annoying friend.

She supposed that was close enough to the truth.

Rounds began promptly at 8:00 a.m. The residents and students were always relieved when the attending physician showed up either on time or a few minutes late. Having the attending show up early caused panicky, last-minute completions of notes and charts. No one wanted to be caught unprepared.

Though this was Ron's first rotation, and first real experience with hospital rounds, he felt more comfortable with the process than he might have expected. He liked the attending quite a bit. Dr. Cudahy was a seasoned hospitalist who was cordial and considerate to her patients and associates. Her first lecture to the three students on this team—Ron, Haley and Hardik Bhatnagar—had included a reminder that all the patients they would see in this facility had spent time serving their country and in return deserved to be treated with gratitude and respect, no matter what unhealthy lifestyle choices they might have made.

Along with his two classmates, three residents, Dr. Cudahy and her nurse, Ron entered the room of the first patient they would be seeing—Haley's flirtatious Mr. Eddington. The thin, wan man winked at Haley, who stood beside his bed to begin her presentation. A warm, answering smile reflected in her amber eyes when she spoke to the assembled group.

Haley was good at presenting, Ron thought with a touch of pride for her. She looked comfortable and confident as she gave a brief summary of Mr. Eddington's condition, his experiences during the night and the resident's plan for continued treatment. She was able to answer the attending's questions with only a glance at her notes, which made both her and her resident look good. Ron gave her a surreptitious thumbs-up when they left the room to move to the next.

Hardik sailed through his presentation of his first patient, but stumbled during his second stop. He'd forgotten to note the new antibiotic that had been started during the night, and as a result, his resident had to step in to answer the attending's questions, leaving Hardik embarrassed. It happened to all of them, of course; Dr. Cudahy even deliberately tried to stump them at times, just to keep them humble and on their toes. Ron still felt bad for his classmate—and hoped he didn't make the same mistakes with his own patients.

Ron kept his presentations brief and to the point, despite his urge to crack a few jokes to make everyone laugh. Which, of course, made him think of Haley's comment that everyone was just waiting for him to display his "real" self during rounds. Had she only been teasing? Or did she really believe the serious and proficient side of him was only an act?

Haley looked good today, he mused, watching her present her final patient. Georgia McMillan, an sixty-eight-year-old retired Air Force nurse, was being treated for pneumonia in addition to emphysema and congestive heart failure, all common to this facility's population. Many of the veterans had been or were still heavy smokers, leading to a high incidence of lung and heart diseases among other smoking-related ailments.

Letting Haley's presentation drift past him, Ron concentrated instead on how fresh and professional she looked in her spotless, short white coat over a melon-colored top with tan pants. Her collar-length, honey-colored hair was neatly restrained with a brown headband, and her makeup was flawless and understated—not that her pretty, girl-next-door face needed much enhancement.

He realized abruptly that the group was moving toward the door, leaving him gazing rather stupidly at Haley. He recovered quickly, sending a smile of gratitude toward the patient who allowed the students to gawk at her and learn from her suffering. Ms. McMillan batted her eyes at him in return, making him chuckle as he stepped out of the room.

When all the patients had been seen, Dr. Cudahy led them to a conference room for a teaching session. The residents and students followed like ducklings trailing a mother duck— which was the way Ron had come to think of them during the past week. Dr. Cudahy had informed them yesterday that she would be discussing hospital-acquired infection today. The students had been expected to research the subject on their own last night so they could participate in an intelligent discussion of the subject. Ron had spent several hours in front of his computer and textbooks, and hoped he would be ready if the attending tried to trip him up with a difficult question.

He took this training more seriously than some people gave him credit for, he thought with another glance at Haley.

Haley was tired when she arrived home, but that was nothing new. She would take the weariness after a long day on the wards any time over the grueling schedule of classes and exams that had made up the first two years of medical school.

Pulling the band from her hair, she shook her head to loosen her tidy bob and headed straight for the kitchen in search of something cold to drink. Her apartment was an older one, and the appliances were almost as old, but at least the aging fridge worked well enough to keep her sodas cold, she thought, taking a big swallow of a diet lemon-lime beverage. The citrusy liquid flooded her throat with a satisfying bite, somewhat reviving her after being out in the heat of an Arkansas late-July afternoon. She'd grown up in this state, so she was accustomed to the oppressive, humid summer temperatures, but she still preferred the crisp, cool days of autumn.

Her phone rang just as she dropped onto her couch to prop up her aching feet for a few minutes before she made dinner. Seeing her mother's number on the ID screen, she smiled when she answered. "Hi, Mom. What's up?"

Haley's parents still lived in Russellville where Haley had grown up, a one-hour or so drive from Haley's Little Rock apartment complex. An only child, she was especially close with her mother, and they talked and saw each other as often as they could considering their hectic schedules. Her parents ran a busy restaurant, Pasta Wright, in Russellville, which kept them both running pretty much 24/7. Haley had worked in that establishment, herself, during her senior year of high school and for two years afterward before starting college, so she knew exactly how hard those days could be, though her parents still loved the work.

Her mom adored hearing about Haley's medical school experiences. Janice Wright had always encouraged her daughter to pursue any career she desired. She wanted Haley always to be able to take care of herself, to be a modern, independent woman with many roads open to her. Haley's dad had been just as encouraging for her to go after her dreams, pushing her out of the restaurant and into college as soon as they were all sure the restaurant venture would survive.

Her parents had offered to support her financially during her medical education by getting another mortgage on the house that was already collateral for their business, but she had refused to allow them to make that sacrifice. She would get by on loans, she assured them. If she was going to be an independent woman, she might as well start now.

"Have you heard any more from that young man you were dating last month?" her mother asked as the conversation wound down. "Kris?"

"No, Mom. I won't be hearing from Kris anymore. I heard he's seeing someone else now."

"And you're really okay with that? You seemed so fond of him."

"I was fond of him. He's a great guy. But it was never serious. We were just friends, hanging out and having a little fun. And it was my decision to go our separate ways. I'm staying busy with this rotation. After this one, I have pediatrics and then surgery, which involves really long hours. I just didn't have the time or energy to devote to Kris—or anyone else—right now."

Haley had known from the start that Kris wouldn't be in her life for long. After dating him only a few months, she had tactfully informed him it wasn't fair to him to continue the way they had been, with her too busy to see him regularly and too distracted by thoughts of school when they were together. When he hadn't even bothered to argue, she'd realized that he was rather relieved she had made that decision for them. It wasn't giving up, she assured herself, when that outcome had been predetermined from the beginning.

"Well—just remember you can't work all the time. Have some fun when you can."

Her mom had warned her several times that, as important as her career might be, it shouldn't be the only thing in Haley's life. One must stay balanced, she counseled, with family and other interests to fill the hours away from work.

"I'll try to take a little time off when I can, Mom."

Not that there was much time to take. Even with the first two years behind her, the next two would be busy in their own way. Long hours in rotations, preparing for Step 2 of the licensure exams, applying and interviewing for residency programs. Becoming the physician she wanted to be.

When the time was right, she would find someone to share her life with, Haley assured herself. In her experience, everything had a way of working out as it was meant to.

Which sentiment would only give Ron more reason to tease her about her "optimistic cheerleader" attitude, she thought with a grimace as she and her mom concluded their call.

She wondered impatiently why thoughts of Ron had popped into her head at just that moment.

As they had vowed to try to do regularly during the remainder of medical school, the study group members met for dinner after work the following week, a rare evening when all five were free for a couple of hours. It still felt odd to Ron not to see his friends in classes every day. Though they stayed in touch, this was the first time they'd all been able to get together to compare notes on their rotations that had started two weeks earlier.

Anne's husband, Liam, and Connor's wife, Mia, had been invited to join them this evening, but Liam was out of town on business, as he so often was, and Mia had opted to see a movie with her stepdaughter, instead. Ron suspected she'd done so to give the group a chance to share tales about their rotation experiences without worrying if they were boring her with their shoptalk.

They sat in a big, round booth with plates of seafood and glasses of wine on the table in front of them. "How are your rotations going?" Ron asked, including everyone in the question.

Connor Hayes spoke first. The father of eight-year-old Alexis, Connor had just celebrated his first wedding anniversary with Mia. Ron had attended that wedding, as had the other members of their group.

"I'm enjoying geriatrics," Connor said. "Had my second hospice visit this afternoon. I can see how much good the hospice teams do for the families in the end stages of their loved ones' lives. I really admire the ones who do it every day, especially the volunteers."

"Are you considering geriatrics now?" Anne asked him.

Smiling, Connor shook his head. "Still planning family practice. It's what I've always wanted to do, and I doubt I'll change my mind during rotations."

"My psych rotation is pretty interesting, but it's not on my list of possible specialties," James Stillman commented. "I don't mind it for this six weeks, but I think I'll be ready to move on to something else by the time the rotation ends."

Twenty-nine-year-old James had already earned a doctorate in microbiology before he'd entered medical school. He had said once that he kept going to school to put off committing to any particular career, a sentiment Ron had laughingly agreed with.

After dropping out of college his first semester after high school, Ron had drifted for a couple of years, trying several unsuccessful jobs before deciding to give college another try. Applying himself to his studies that time, he had done well enough in his classes—particularly his science classes—that his faculty advisor had encouraged him to consider medical school. Ron had taken the MCAT, the medical school admissions exam, half expecting he wouldn't do well enough to even be considered. No one had been more startled than him when he'd received a very high score.

Well—maybe his family had been more surprised. His dad had predicted Ron would drop out of medical school when it got too tough. His mother had worried aloud that Ron wasn't doctor material, and that he'd only been setting himself up for disappointment. None of his siblings thought he'd ever make anything of himself; they'd expected him to settle for the same aimless and unfulfilling existence they led themselves.

He'd made it through the interviews and had been placed on the alternates list for admission. Even then, he'd waited to be told that he hadn't made it in. Apparently, enough first-choice applicants had declined to open up a slot for him. Rather dazed to have gotten that far, he'd secured his loans and shown up for classes—only to be slammed by the reality of the commitment he had made when he found out just how hard medical school really was. He'd been unprepared for the long hours, the constant stress, the sleep deprivation, the massive amounts of information he had been expected to learn and access on demand. Several times, he'd almost chucked it all and taken to his heels.

Only a few things had kept him on course. His pride, which had made him reluctant to admit to his family that they'd been right about him not being cut out to be a doctor. His deep desire to enter a career in which he felt he could make a difference in other people's lives. And the people of his close-knit and incredibly encouraging study group—including Haley, whose refusal to let anyone around her concede defeat had been as inspiring as it was irritating at times.

Maybe at the back of his mind he'd kept the comforting thought that he could always move on to something else if this didn't work out. His life wouldn't end if he didn't become a doctor. He'd survive if he didn't pass the next test, or score high enough on Step 1 of the national medical licensing exam. But somehow, he'd continued to pass—maybe not with the highest grades in the class, but respectably enough to remain in good standing. And he'd passed Step 1, news he had learned only days earlier. So, it seemed that he might just become a doctor, after all.

Amazing.

"If not psychiatry, have you given any more thought to what type of medicine you want to practice, James?" Haley asked curiously. "Have you narrowed the choices down since the last time we all got together?"

Connor was the only one in the group who seemed certain about his area of specialty. He'd intended from the start to practice family medicine. Anne had entered school saying she wanted to be a surgeon like her father, grandfather and brother; now she said she might be interested in obstetrics and gynecology, which would include some surgery.

James, Haley and Ron had all kept their options open, for various reasons. Ron because he simply didn't know, yet, what he wanted to do. He hoped he'd figure it out sometime during rotations. He had less than a year and a half before he would start interviewing for residency programs.

James smiled wryly in response to Haley's question. "Who knows? Maybe I'll enter law school after I've earned this degree."

Everyone laughed, as James obviously expected, but Ron wondered if there was any truth in the threat. Though Ron considered James one of his two closest male friends, he had to admit he didn't always know what was going on in James's head. James was friendly, generous, easy to talk to, always supportive—but private to the extent that even his friends weren't always sure they knew him very well. Ron wouldn't be surprised by anything James decided to do after medical school—even law school.

"What about you, Ron?" Connor asked, distracting him from his musings about James. "Reached any decisions yet?"

Ron shrugged. "Still thinking pediatrics. Or maybe geriatrics."

Connor laughed. "Quite the range there."

Smiling sheepishly, Ron nodded. "Yeah. I like kids and seniors. You can count on both of them to tell you what they're really thinking."

"Not to mention that both groups always laugh at your silly jokes," Haley pointed out.

He grinned at her. "There's that, too."

"How's it going on the VA wards?" James included both Haley and Ron in the question as he reached for his wineglass.

Ron spoke before Haley had the chance. "Haley's excelling, of course. The most prepared, most eager and most helpful medical student on the rotation. Her resident loves her."

Haley sighed gustily in response to Ron's teasing.

James chuckled. "I have to admit, I miss Haley's motivational minispeeches when I try to study by myself in the evenings to prepare for the next day's sessions."

Haley smiled at him. "Just give me a call whenever you need a motivating speech. I always have one or two prepared."

"I'll do that." James smiled back at her, and Ron found himself having to smooth a frown, for some reason.

"Darn it." Anne scowled down at her lap, into which she had just dropped a bite of her entrée. "Now I've got a splatter of sauce on my skirt. Of course it missed the napkin entirely."

"I've got one of those stain removal pens in my purse," Haley offered immediately. "Let's go to the ladies' room and I'll help you."

Anne slid toward the edge of the booth. "Thanks, Haley."

Standing to let Anne out, Ron nodded wryly. "That's our Haley. Always prepared for anything."

Haley punched him in the arm when she passed him on the way to the restroom with Anne. Rubbing the stinging spot ruefully, he chuckled as he returned to his seat.

"How are the two of you getting along on the wards?" Connor asked, having watched the interplay.

"Fine," Ron assured him. "Now that some of the pressure of exams are behind us, she's a lot more relaxed. Not as touchy."

Both Connor and James looked at him with raised eyebrows.

"What?"

"You're blaming those last few months of conflict on Haley?" James asked skeptically.

"Well, maybe not all of it." Ron took a sip of his beer to avoid meeting his friends' eyes. "Maybe I teased her a couple of times when she wasn't in the mood for joking."

"And maybe you made a few cutting remarks about her boyfriend," Connor murmured into his own glass.

"Ex-boyfriend," Ron corrected with a scowl. "The guy was a doormat. Followed Haley around like a puppy. No personality of his own at all. I don't know what she ever saw in him in the first place."

The other two men exchanged an amused glance, and Ron figured they were thinking of Kris's dimples or muscles or some of the other superficial attributes that had probably attracted Haley to the guy. Feeling his good mood begin to disintegrate, he quickly changed the subject, sharing a funny story from the wards. He was both pleased and relieved when his friends laughed and contributed a couple of amusing stories from their own experiences during the past couple of weeks, all being careful to follow privacy rules and not mention names or specifics about their patients.

Medical anecdotes he could handle. Talking about Haley and her good-looking ex-boyfriend—not so much.

"I'm glad you're feeling better today, Ms. McMillan." Haley smiled at the former Air Force nurse who sat in a recliner in a private room, snugly wrapped in a hospital blanket. She was still on supplemental oxygen as well as the antibiotics dripping into the IV tubing connected to her left arm, but her condition had improved considerably during the night. "It's good that you feel well enough to sit up for a while."

"Feels good to get out of that bed," Georgia McMillan agreed with a firm nod of her gray head, followed by a rattling cough. Catching her breath, she eyed Haley narrowly. "Don't smoke, do you?"

"No, ma'am."

"Good. Don't start." She coughed more forcefully while Haley studied her chart.

"I won't. Are you okay?"

Catching her breath, the patient waved off Haley's question with one thin hand. "I'm as okay as I ever am these days. Feel a whole lot better than I did when I was admitted, anyway."

"That's good to hear." Haley jotted a couple of notes on the back of Ms. McMillan's H & P, then folded the paper and stuck it into her coat pocket.

"You look like you got some rest last night."

A little surprised by the comment, Haley glanced up from the patient chart. "Yes, I slept very well, thank you."

"I remember my medical training. Ain't easy, is it?"

Chuckling, she pulled her stethoscope from another pocket. "No, ma'am, it isn't."

"Just hope you never have to practice in a tent with shells exploding around you."

"I can't imagine working under those conditions."

Georgia enjoyed talking about her experiences in a war zone and Haley usually liked listening to the stories.

Unfortunately, she was running a little behind this morning because of complications with one of her other two patients, and she was beginning to worry she wouldn't have her notes completed in time for rounds. She mentally crossed her fingers that Dr. Cudahy wouldn't choose today to show up early.

She was just preparing to leave the room when Georgia startled her yet again. "Has that boy asked you out yet?"

Haley paused in midstep toward the door. "Which boy is that, Ms. McMillan?"

"That cute blondish student with the sexy smile. The one who's always grinning at you."

Haley laughed self-consciously. "You mean Ron? He's a friend. A classmate. We aren't—"

"You might not be, but he is," Georgia cut in with a wicked smile that showed a hint of the saucy young woman she'd once been.

Smiling wryly, Haley shook her head. "You don't see the way he acts when we're not on rounds. He goes to great lengths to tease and torment me."

Her patient nodded as if Haley had just confirmed her theory. "Men are still just big boys at heart. That's his way of letting you know he's got a crush on you."

"Oh, I don't think so."

"I watch him while you're giving your presentations on rounds. He can't take his eyes from you."

Haley was growing accustomed to odd and sometimes inappropriate comments from her patients, but for some reason, this conversation flustered her. "He's just paying attention, Ms. McMillan. That's the whole point of our rounds, so we'll learn about the various conditions of the patients we're seeing."

"Hmm. The other student pays attention, too, but not the same way that boy does. You mark my words, he's got it bad for you. Don't you be surprised when he makes his move. And if I were you, I'd take him up on it. Nice-looking young doctor with a sense of humor and kind eyes—a girl could do a whole lot worse, let me tell you. As someone who's been married three times, I know a bit about winners and losers," she added with a phlegmy cackle.

"Well, I, um—" Haley gave her patient a strained smile. "I've got to run, Ms. McMillan. I'll see you again in a little while during rounds."

The woman nodded, looking tired when her impish smile faded. "Send my nurse in here, will you? Think I'm ready to get back in that bed, after all."

"I will."

Haley made her escape, letting out a whoosh of breath when the door closed behind her. She had to find a nurse, locate an available computer, type her notes and be ready for rounds in just under twenty minutes.

She had a feeling she would have to make a massive effort not to be distracted by Georgia McMillan's outrageous comments while she tried to concentrate on her work. The woman had to be mistaken that she'd seen anything meaningful in the way Ron looked at her. Probably just entertaining herself with some romantic imagining. Because it couldn't possibly be true that Ron had feelings for her—could it?

Swallowing hard, Haley pushed that unsettling question to the back of her mind and hurried to find Ms. McMillan's nurse.

Chapter Two

Late Thursday afternoon, after a long day of morning rounds and an afternoon spent being a resident's minion, Haley gathered her things in preparation for heading home. She didn't have to report in that weekend, and she planned to spend the next two days doing laundry, catching up on housework and preparing for next week's lectures. That would be her last week on wards; after that, she would move to internal medicine outpatient clinic for four weeks before beginning her pediatrics rotation.

But before starting pediatrics, she had to pass the internal medicine board exam, or the "shelf exam," she reminded herself. Which meant more cramming. She was aware that she would spend the rest of her professional life continuing her education and being tested on her knowledge, but that was okay. It was part of the career she'd chosen, and she knew how important it was for a physician to stay current on the newest procedures and treatments. At least she'd be earning a living, rather than going further into debt, once she completed her fourth year of medical school.

Ron fell into step beside her when she headed for the elevator. Her medical student white coat was still spotless and crisp, even after a hard day's work. The roomy pockets were full, but neatly organized. Ron's coat was rather wrinkled, his pockets crammed with instruments, notes and medical reference materials. The coat had looked exactly the same way when he'd arrived that morning. Beneath it, his blue dress shirt was correspondingly crumpled, his red-print tie slightly askew and his khaki slacks creased at the knees. Though he was clean shaven, his disheveled sandy hair fell boyishly over his forehead, making him look a bit younger than his twenty-seven years.

The rumpled look certainly worked for him. For some reason, rather than unprofessional or scruffy, he looked appealing and earnest, like a man who had more on his mind than vanity. She was well aware of the way other women smiled at him when he passed them in the hallways. Ron might not be as movie-star handsome as their friend James, but Ron had a sexy charm of his own that he didn't hesitate to fall back on when necessary.

Not that she was at all susceptible to that charm, she assured herself. She knew him too well to step into that snare.

"Long day, huh?" he asked as he reached around her to press the elevator call button. His arm brushed hers with the movement, and she stepped a bit too quickly away, earning a quizzical look from him.

"Yes," she said, shifting her purse strap higher on her shoulder, vaguely hoping he'd think her retreat had been due to a slipping bag. Glancing around to make sure no one could overhear, she added, "Paulsen was in a mood this morning, wasn't he?"

"No kidding. Thought he was going to chew a piece off poor Hardik's hide."

"I'm glad I got Dr. Carr for my resident. I work very well with him."

"Yeah. I get along fine with Dr. Prickett. Just Hardik's bad luck that he got Paulsen."

Everyone knew there were some residents and attendings who enjoyed their power a little too much, especially when it came to abusing med students, nurses and lowly interns. Paulsen was one of the difficult ones. The power hierarchy in a teaching hospital was rigidly layered, often repressing and politically complicated, and it wasn't hard to get on a superior's bad side. Haley was relieved that she'd drawn a more patient, if perpetually harried, resident for her first rotation.

The elevator doors opened to an empty car, and they stepped in. Haley leaned against the far wall from Ron, appreciating the support. She really was tired. Her empty stomach reminded her that she'd been able to take only a few minutes for a quick lunch earlier, and she hoped she had something in her kitchen to eat that wouldn't require much preparation.

"Want to go have some coffee?" Ron asked during their descent to the lobby. "I could use some caffeine before I start prepping for tomorrow's didactic."

"Um...coffee?"

"Yeah. James is meeting me at the usual place in a few minutes. I thought you might like to join us."

"Oh. You and James."

Ron frowned at her. "Is something wrong, Haley? You're acting kind of odd today."

Drawing herself straighter, she shook her head. "No, I'm fine. Just kind of brain-dead after a draining day."

And then, to further convince him that nothing at all had changed between them...and why should it have?...she said brightly, "I'd love to have coffee with you and James. I'll meet you there."

He still looked at her as though something puzzled him, but she kept her smile in place as she headed for her car. Only when she was buckled into the driver's seat did she allow it to fade. What was she doing, letting a random comment from a fanciful patient interfere with her friendship with her study pal? She and Ron had had their share of conflict, but romantic yearnings had never been an issue. Their problems were due entirely to conflicting personality traits, all the more reason to put Georgia's mistaken observations and unsolicited advice out of her mind.

She must be more tired than she had realized. She could use a cup of coffee and a few laughs with her friends.

Because Haley was delayed by a red light, Ron was the first to reach the coffee shop. He was already placing his order when she got in line, and had secured a small table when she joined him with her skinny vanilla latte. "Looks like we beat James here," she commented, slipping into a plastic chair.

"Looks like."

Ron took a cautious sip of his own hot drink. "I was tempted by those muffins, but I figured I'd better eat some real food first," he said after swallowing. "Had a sandwich and some chips for lunch, but they're long since worn off."

"I got half a salad down before I had to run help my resident with something," she admitted. "I'm starving."

"Want to go next door for Chinese after we finish these? We'll see if James wants to join us."

The fast-food Chinese place next door was good, quick and relatively inexpensive, all points in its favor. Haley nodded. "Sure. I've got time for some noodles before I hit the books."

"Great. I'm not in the mood to cook for myself tonight."

"Neither am I." She sipped her coffee, trying to decide whether she should repeat her conversation with Georgia to him. Ron would probably get a kick out of the older woman's misguided matchmaking efforts. He loved to share amusing stories. But for some reason, she kept the patient's observations to herself. Maybe they hadn't been all that funny, after all. Just…mistaken.

They chatted about their workday for a few minutes more before being interrupted by the chirp of Ron's phone. He slipped it from its belt holder and glanced at the screen. "Text from James. He's not going to be joining us, after all."

"Oh? Nothing's wrong, I hope."

"No. Just having trouble with his car again."

James's classic sports car was notorious for mechanical problems, about which the study group had teased him often.

Ron shook his head as he returned the phone to its holder after sending an acknowledgment of the message. "Don't know why he doesn't give up on that car and buy a new one."

"He loves that old car." The car seemed to be the only inanimate object James did truly value. He'd even given it a name. Terri. If there was any personal significance to the name, he'd never said.

"Way more trouble than it's worth. I'd have dumped it a long time ago."

But then, that was Ron's stated philosophy, Haley mused, gazing into her coffee cup. If something didn't work out, or was more trouble than he deemed worthwhile, he walked away without looking back. He'd even proclaimed that he was prepared to do the same with medical school. If his grades had slipped or he'd failed one of the critical tests, he'd have taken it as a sign to move on, he'd insisted.

Haley had made no effort to hide her disapproval of that attitude. She was of the "Try, try again" credo herself. Ron had teased her during their first year of studying together that "Never give up. Never surrender!" should be her motto. The allusion had sailed over her head until he'd hosted the study group one blessedly study-free Saturday afternoon for pizza and a showing of a sci-fi spoof movie that was one of his favorite films. He'd performed a bowing, fist-against-the-heart salute every time he'd seen her for several months afterward, until she'd finally threatened to dropkick his computer if he kept it up. Although he hadn't believed her—entirely—he'd finally grown tired of the joke and moved on to another one.

He drained his coffee. "Ready for noodles?"

She'd already agreed to eat with him. It would be a little too obvious to cancel just because James wasn't coming along, after all. Besides, why shouldn't she share a quick meal with Ron? She could only blame Georgia McMillan and her silly imaginings for making her suddenly self-conscious around her friend.

Telling herself this foolishness would all be forgotten by tomorrow, she pushed her empty coffee cup aside and reached for her purse.

Ron couldn't quite figure out what it was, but something was off with Haley. She seemed to be lost somewhere in her own thoughts, though she made an effort to participate in their conversation. He couldn't read the expression in her eyes, and her smiles looked a little distant. She didn't seem annoyed with him—a common enough occurrence that he knew how to recognize those signs—but neither was she fully connecting with him this evening.

Setting down his chopsticks, he studied her from across the little table in the crowded Chinese restaurant. "What's going on, Haley?"

She frowned. "I don't know what you mean."

"You're acting weird. Have been ever since we left work today. Have I done something to tick you off again?"

She twisted noodles on her own disposable chopsticks, and he wondered if she was deliberately avoiding his gaze. "Have I ever not let you know when you've ticked me off?" she asked wryly.

"Well, no. But I think I know you well enough to tell when something is bothering you. Did something happen at work today?"

"Not…exactly."

"What does that mean?"

She sighed a little and looked up from her bowl. "One of my patients said something that caught me a little off guard, but it's no big deal, okay? It was just an observation she made that I think was inaccurate."

Conscious of the patient privacy laws that had been drilled into them, he glanced around to make sure no one could hear them before leaning a little closer to respond. "The only 'she' you have is the one who always winks at me when we come into her room on rounds. What did she say?"

Haley shook her head. "You know we're not supposed to discuss our patients outside the hospital."

"Not if it's a privacy issue," he agreed. "Is that what it was? Is there something your resident should know, and you're wondering how to tell him?"

She shook her head again. "It's nothing like that. She was just teasing me. Let it go, Ron, okay?"

"Fine." He wondered if she would have been so reticent with Anne. Or even James or Connor. But then he told himself to stop taking it so personally that she was holding something back from him. It wasn't as if they told each other everything.

He'd become increasingly aware lately that there were a lot of things he didn't understand about Haley. One would think after knowing her for two years, he'd have learned all there was to discover. And yet, it felt sometimes as if he'd barely scratched the surface of Haley Wright.

She gave another little shake of her head, as if clearing her mind of whatever had been bothering her, and quickly changed the subject. "I met with the rest of the class officers this morning for another planning session for the big tailgate party in September. I think it's going to be a lot of fun."

Haley was the class vice president, and an active member of several committees. The whole class had been together every day during the first two years of classes and lectures; now that rotations had started, they would rarely all be in one place again. Haley was committed to making sure the class stayed connected as much as possible during these final two years of medical school. If it were up to her, they'd probably have monthly pep rallies designed to keep up morale and increase classmate bonding, he thought with a smothered grin.

"You are planning to go, aren't you?" she asked when he didn't immediately respond.

He shrugged. "Probably. I figure you'll come after me if I don't show up."

She smiled. "You could be right."

She had a pretty smile. It was one of the first things he'd noticed about her when they'd met. She'd sat beside him in their first class and their hands had collided when they'd both reached to plug in their computers to the same outlet. She'd smiled, and his heart had given a funny thump. He still remembered their first conversation.

"Aren't you excited?" she had asked.

"I guess."

"And a little nervous?"

He'd had no intention of letting her see that he was scared spitless. He had shrugged and drawled, "Nah. I figure if I bomb at doctoring, I can always become a mortician."

Haley had blinked a couple of times, then smiled again. "We aren't going to bomb. Not if we give it all we've got. Maybe we can work together sometime. We'll find a few others who want to form a study group."

He had realized immediately that he was sitting next to a cheerleader. It had been no surprise to learn in coming months that she had, indeed, been a cheerleader throughout school—not to mention senior class president, "Most Likely to Succeed" and a homecoming princess. Far from being one of the "mean girls," Haley had probably been popular with everyone in her school. Teachers, other students, cafeteria workers, custodians—she'd have been equally pleasant to all of them, and she would have had their vote for any position she ran for. She just had that way about her.

There'd been times when her we-can-do-anything attitude had irked him. Especially when his own confidence and morale had been lowest. When he'd been convinced he would have to drop out of medical school and return to east Arkansas with his tail between his legs, proving his family right in their predictions that he would never make it all the way through.

It hadn't taken him long to find the right tone to chip through Haley's cheery optimism. He seemed to have a knack for setting off her temper, which most people probably never even saw. Yet as much as they irritated each other at times, he wasn't at all sure he'd have made it through those first two years without her. And the rest of the study group members, too, he amended quickly.

They talked about the tailgate party plans for a few minutes, and then Haley set down her chopsticks. "I can't eat any more. I'd better go home and study."

"Yeah, me, too. You know, you could come over to my place. We could have some dessert, study a couple hours."

She had studied at his apartment many times during the past two years. He wasn't sure she'd ever been there without any other members of their study group, but it wouldn't be so different with just the two of them, right? Just because he and Haley were the only ones of their group on this rotation didn't mean they couldn't still be study partners.

So why did she look so surprised by his suggestion? "Um—your place?"

He cocked an eyebrow at her. "Yeah. You remember—the loft apartment with the bare gray walls? The couch you said looks like it came through World War II—and lost?"

She sighed. "I remember your apartment. I was just...I really need to go home. I have to do laundry tonight or I'll be doing rounds in cutoffs and a T-shirt tomorrow. Maybe we can study together another night?"

Something was definitely on Haley's mind, but he suspected it would do him no good to ask her again what was bothering her. He simply nodded and stood to escort her to the door. They were both parked in front of the coffee shop; he accompanied her down the sidewalk to her car.

He placed a hand on her shoulder to detain her when she opened her car door and prepared to climb in. "Haley—"

She glanced at his hand, then his face. "Yes?"

"You know if there's anything bothering you, I'm here for you, right? I mean, if you want to talk or if there's anything you need..."

She went very still for a moment, then made a face, looking more like herself than she had all evening. "Thanks, Ron. I don't know what's wrong with me tonight. Just tired, I guess. Really, everything's fine. But thanks for the concern."

He searched her face, relieved to see that the smile was back in her eyes now. "You're sure?"

"I'm sure. Really. Just tired."

He chuckled. "Show me a medical student who isn't tired."

The smile in her eyes traveled to her lips, which tilted infectiously. "So true."

His fingers tightened spasmodically on her shoulder. He loosened them quickly, turning the gesture into a friendly little pat. "Still, if there's anything you need, you've got my number."

"Thanks, Ron." After a momentary hesitation, she smiled again and slid into her car. "See you tomorrow."

"Yeah." He stepped back quickly, narrowly missing having her car door slammed on his fingers. "See ya," he murmured, watching her drive away.

Ron was passing an open hospital room door the next afternoon when a voice stopped him. "Hey. Dr. Gibson."

Frowning in confusion, he paused and looked around, wondering if he'd misheard.

"*Psst.* Dr. Gibson."

Following the sound of the woman's voice, he stepped curiously into the open doorway. Wrapped in a thin white blanket, Georgia McMillan sat in a recliner near the windows, facing the hallway so she could watch people go by outside her room. An IV stand sat at one side of her chair, two bags dripping into the tubes inserted in her thin arm. On the other side of the chair, an oxygen tank pumped air into the tubes in her nose.

Her breathing rasped in the quiet room, but her smile was impish when she saw that she had his attention. "How's it going, cutie?"

He grinned. "Fine, thank you, Ms. McMillan. And you?"

"Still hanging in."

"Is there something I can do for you?"

She crooked a bony finger at him, inviting him into the room. Thinking of the list of tasks his resident had given him to complete within the next hour, he entered. She was probably just a little lonely. As far as he had observed, Ms. McMillan had no family. She wasn't one of the three patients he'd been assigned—she was Haley's responsibility—but since he saw her every morning on team rounds, she wasn't a complete stranger to him.

"How are you feeling?" he asked her.

She waved off the question impatiently. "Same as always. Must be better, though, they're letting me out of here tomorrow."

"That's good to hear." She would be back, he knew, and probably soon. It was obvious even to a third-year student that her health was deteriorating.

"How's your life outside of work?" she asked, her gaze locked on his face. "You got a girlfriend?"

He chuckled. "No, ma'am, not at the moment. I don't have time for one."

"Nonsense. There's always time for a personal life. Don't let your job consume you."

"I'll try not to."

"What about that other pretty medical student? Haley? She's not seeing anyone, either. I asked her."

"What about her, Ms. McMillan?"

"Why don't you ask her out? I really like her."

"Well, yes, so do I, but Haley and I are just friends."

She waved her unsteady hand again. "My third husband was my best friend. Only one of my marriages that lasted. We'd still be married today if he hadn't flipped over his tractor while he was mowing a steep hill. I lost him four years ago. Still miss the silly puns he was always coming up with."

"I'm sorry about your loss, ma'am."

She nodded, then shrugged. "Just shows, you have to make the most of every moment. Me and Joe did that. We had a good twelve years together."

"I'm glad you have those nice memories of him. But Haley and I aren't—"

She gave a wheezy laugh. "You're thinking I'm a nosy old biddy, and you're right. Ain't like I've got anything else to do in here but watch the staff and speculate about their private lives. I like Haley. She's a sweetheart. And since I'm leaving here tomorrow and neither of you are working this weekend, I probably won't get another chance to meddle with the two of you."

"Ms. McMillan—"

"Take my advice, young man. Give that one a chance. She's a keeper."

He smiled, both amused and unnerved by the woman's persistence. He really did like kids and seniors, even when their artless observations startled him at times. "I'll keep your suggestion in mind, ma'am."

She nodded in satisfaction. "You do that."

"I really have to get back to work. Is there anything you need before I go?"

"No. That silly girl will be in here in a few minutes. The nurse's aide. Talks a mile a minute, and giggles between every other word. Good at her job, though," she added grudgingly.

"Okay. Have a good night, Ms. McMillan. It's been a pleasure to meet you. I hope you continue to do well after you return home tomorrow."

She shrugged, an acknowledgment of what they both knew about her prognosis. "You're a nice young man. You're going to be a damned good doctor. Good husband material, too."

Chuckling, he moved toward the door. He'd have to tell Haley about this conversation. She'd get a kick out of—

He stopped abruptly in the doorway. With a slight frown, he turned to the patient again. "Ms. McMillan, you haven't said anything to Haley about this, have you? About her and me, I mean?"

He could tell the answer from her expression.

"I might have mentioned that you seem like a good catch to me. And that you might be interested in her, judging from the way you look at her."

"Huh. Well, maybe you shouldn't mention anything like that again. Okay?"

She shrugged. "I'm leaving tomorrow, anyway. Probably won't see her again. Just thought I'd plant a seed in a couple of young minds before I go."

Giving her a little wave of farewell, Ron left the room. He didn't realize he was scowling as he stalked down the hallway until a young volunteer jumped out of his way, looking warily at him when he passed.

Smoothing his expression, he pushed Ms. McMillan's words to the back of his mind. He had work to do now. But he would be having a talk with Haley before the night was over.

Chapter Three

Haley sat at her table Friday evening reading an online medical article when someone rapped sharply on her door. She wasn't expecting company and almost never had drop-by visitors, so the sound startled her. Though she'd shed her comfortable black flats, she still wore the pearl-colored summer sweater and pale gray slacks she'd donned for work, so at least she was decently dressed for company. Leaving the article on the computer screen, she walked across the living room and looked curiously through the peephole in the door.

"Ron?" Surprised, she opened the door. "What's up?"

A frown creased his sandy brows and darkened his blue eyes. "Mind if I come in?"

He'd never dropped by without calling before; as far as she could remember, he'd never been there without the rest of the study group. Speculation about the reason for this visit made her hesitate a moment before answering.

His frown deepened. "Is this a bad time?"

He glanced beyond her, as though checking to see if she had other visitors.

"No, it's fine." She moved out of his way. "Come in."

He walked to the center of the living room. Studying him somewhat warily, she closed the door. It wasn't the first time she'd seen Ron in a bad mood, but it had been a while.

"Have a seat," she said, waving toward the cushioned, cream-colored couch she'd bought for comfort as much for style. Her whole apartment was furnished with relaxation in mind; in addition to the couch, the living room featured a cushy green recliner, a brown leather club chair she'd found at an estate sale and trendily mismatched tables arranged for her guests' convenience. She enjoyed entertaining, though she'd had little time for it since starting medical school, only hosting her study group on occasion. "Can I get you anything?"

He shook his head. "I was going to talk to you at the hospital, but you avoided me all afternoon."

"I didn't avoid you." Of course, she hadn't exactly gone looking for him, either, she admitted silently.

He pushed his hands into the pockets of his rumpled khaki slacks. "So it was just an accident that you were everywhere I wasn't today?"

Feeling defensive now, she planted her hands on her hips. "I saw you on rounds this morning. I was very busy this afternoon. I'm sorry if that was inconvenient for you. What was it you wanted to talk to me about?"

"I visited one of your patients this afternoon. Georgia McMillan."

"Oh." She swallowed hard. "What made you do that?"

"She summoned me into her room when I was passing in the hallway."

She knew Georgia enjoyed watching people pass in the hall, occasionally calling out greetings, so it was no surprise that she'd taken advantage of spotting Ron. Unfortunately. "Um—what did she say to you?"

"She wanted to give me some advice about my personal life."

Haley sighed. She didn't really have to ask what advice the romantically minded older woman had offered. "Yes, well, she seems to enjoy doing that."

"Damn it, Haley."

Defensiveness returned, crowding out embarrassment. It wasn't as if she had any control over what her patient said when she wasn't around. "What?"

"We've been friends for two years. Good friends, despite the rough patches."

She nodded. "Yes, we have."

"And you're going to let one old woman's ramblings drive a wedge between us now? After all the other obstacles our friendship has survived?"

He sounded genuinely angry, which—as always—triggered her own rare temper. It seemed to be a unique talent of his. "I'm doing no such thing."

He was pacing now, though her small living space gave him room to take only three or four steps in each direction. "I knew something was bugging you yesterday. Couldn't figure out why you weren't meeting my eyes, why you jumped every time we made accidental contact. Why you started stuttering when I suggested we go to my place. To *study,* damn it."

Two "damn its" in as many minutes. He really was irked.

"I told you I had to do laundry."

"Yeah. And I'd never seen anyone look so eager to spend an evening with detergent and fabric softeners."

"Look, Ron—"

He stopped in front of her, his gaze holding hers. "What I want to know is, why did you let what she said get to you that way? How come you didn't come to me and laugh about it, the way we always do when something funny happens at work?"

"I don't know," she admitted with a sigh. "I just—okay, you're right. I let her get to me. It embarrassed me, and I wasn't sure how to—what to—well, you know."

"What did she say that was so embarrassing?" He looked genuinely perplexed. "All she said to me was that you're a sweetheart and I should ask you out. She giggled a little, and I grinned back at her. I thought you and I would get a laugh out of it, but then I realized that she must have said something similar to you yesterday. And that the unsettling patient comment you mentioned last night must have been hers. So what did she say to you that was so disconcerting?"

She had no intention of telling him Georgia had implied that Ron was in love with her. Sure, they should be able to laugh about that—but for some reason, Haley didn't find it all that funny. "She just went on about what a good catch you are and how I should make an effort to land you. As if you were a prized fish or something. I tried to tell her you and I are good friends, but she just wouldn't let it go. I guess that conversation was still on my mind when you suggested we have coffee and dinner."

"And when I invited you to my place to study."

"I really did need to do laundry," she muttered, glancing down at her hands, which were now clenched in front of her.

He shook his head. "I still don't understand why it shook you up so much for her to suggest I've got a thing for you. I thought it was funny."

It was only natural, she assured herself, that her feminine ego would be a little piqued by that. "I guess I was just more tired than I realized."

The prevarication didn't seem to satisfy him completely, but he nodded. "So we're good, then?"

She gave him a smile she hoped looked completely natural. "Of course we are."

To her relief, he smiled in return, his usual good humor returning to his warm blue eyes. "You don't think I'm going to lure you to my lair so I can jump your bones?"

She sighed gustily, her usual response to his teasing. "No, Ron, I don't think you're going to jump my bones," she said drily, making him laugh.

"Good. Now that that's settled, can I have a sandwich?"

She blinked a couple of times, then glanced toward the table, where a barely touched ham sandwich still sat on a plate next to her computer. "Of course. Sit down, I'll make you one."

Sensing that she needed a change of subject, he talked about work while she moved around the small kitchen, assembling another sandwich and adding a handful of chips and pickles to the plate. She set the plate and a glass of lemonade in front of him, then took her own seat as she responded to his conversational lead. It was much easier to concentrate on their training than…well, other things.

Because he was there and they were already talking about school, it seemed only logical to spend some time studying together after they'd eaten. Their lecture on the following Monday would be about antibiotic-resistant, hospital-acquired infections, so they discussed the topic together, quizzing each other on their knowledge so they would be prepared if their attending physician aimed questions at either of them.

Settling into their practiced study routine, Haley was able to relax and put the former awkwardness aside, to her relief. Ron fell back into teasing, to which she responded with her usual retorts.

As so often was the case, she picked up the information a bit more quickly than Ron—memorization just came easier to her than to him, though once he internalized the material, he retained it well. When she sensed he was becoming frustrated, she tactfully boosted his morale by reminded him how well he'd been doing in the rotation. Clinical skills were his strong point; the fact that he struggled a bit more with the memorization just meant everyone had different learning styles and strengths, which she had lectured more than once during the past two years.

When both were satisfied they were prepared for Monday's lecture, Ron glanced at his watch and stood to leave. "Thanks for the sandwich. And the study help," he added, moving toward the door.

She walked with him so she could lock up behind him. "You helped me, too," she assured him. "It's always easier to study with someone."

Rounding the end of the couch to join him at the door, she stumbled over a strap of the computer bag she'd left lying on the floor. She threw out a hand to steady herself, bumping against the lamp on the end table. She had no trouble preventing a fall, but the hematite bracelet she'd donned that morning caught on the lamp. Shiny, gray-black stones scattered at her feet when the elastic cording snapped.

"Darn it." She bent to scoop up stones, sweeping one hand beneath the couch to retrieve a couple that had tumbled under there.

Ron helped her, plucking a stone from beneath the end table, another from the top of the table. "I don't see any more."

"Thanks." She shook her head. "Clumsy of me."

"Can you have the bracelet restrung?"

"I'll restring it myself when I have time. Kris gave it to me. The stones are hematite—supposed to be calming and grounding."

"Oh." He dropped the stones he held into her open hand as if they'd suddenly turned hot. She knew he'd never cared for Kris. She'd always assumed it was simply a personality clash.

"Okay, I'm off. See you Monday. Have a good weekend."

"You, too." She caught the door when he opened it, preparing to lock it behind him.

Ron turned on the step outside her ground-floor apartment, the familiar look in his eyes warning her that he was going to say something outrageous. "Hey, Haley?"

Her lips twitched. "Yes, Ron?"

"To make it clear—I find your bones totally jumpable. Just don't want to do anything to mess up a good friendship, you know?"

"Um—" She had no idea how she was supposed to respond to that.

Laughing, he turned and walked away.

After a moment, she shook her head, then shut the door with a bit more force than necessary.

Trust Ron to make such an odd joke out of a situation that had already been awkward enough, she thought with a sigh of exasperation.

She spent the rest of the evening wondering at random times if Ron really found her "jumpable."

Rounds on Monday morning went very well. Haley and Hardik had no difficulty with their patient presentations, and Ron sailed through his. To Haley's relief, Ron was his usual self, cutting up with everyone equally, treating her as he always did. There was no more talk of bone-jumping or self-consciousness. Georgia McMillan had been released on Saturday, so they weren't subjected to her blatant matchmaking. Telling herself it had been only a temporary glitch in their friendship, Haley was assured they could put it behind them and go on as they had been.

She was very busy that afternoon, practically running from one assigned task to another, taking only a half hour for a lunch break. She didn't see Ron until late in the afternoon. She had just stepped into the students' room to type up some notes when he walked in.

"Hi, Ron, how's your afternoon...oh, my gosh, what happened?"

Though she remembered that he'd worn a white shirt, red tie and gray slacks beneath his white coat that morning, he wore blue hospital-issue scrubs now. His expression was so grim she knew something must have gone very wrong for him.

The spots of dark color on his cheeks indicated either anger or embarrassment, maybe a mixture of both. He spoke from between clenched teeth. "I screwed up. Big-time. Damn it."

Pushing herself out of the computer chair, she took a step toward him. "What did you do?"

"Dr. Cudahy let me remove a patient's central line. I've done that a couple of times before with my preceptor, so I felt pretty confident. Thought I'd impress the attending and the resident. Like an idiot, I pulled out the line—and forgot to put pressure on the site."

Haley winced, imagining the arterial blood spurt that would have resulted. "I hope you and the patient were the only ones in the vicinity?"

"Oh, no. That would have been bad enough, of course, but Drs. Cudahy and Prickett were standing close enough at the time that we all got splattered. Prickett and I were wearing paper gowns, so only our collars and pants were hit, but Dr. Cudahy thought she was standing far enough away to be safe. She wasn't. She got sprayed. She had to go change into scrubs."

Haley could imagine how humiliated Ron must be feeling right now. It was bad enough to make a mistake in front of a resident, but even more galling to have the attending be both a witness to and a victim of the error.

She was tempted to remind Ron that she'd warned him to be more serious and resist his natural inclination to perform. But this wasn't the time for I-told-you-so. Right now, he just needed a friend.

She rested a hand on his arm. "I'm sorry, Ron. I know that must have been embarrassing. But everyone makes mistakes. Dr. Cudahy and Dr. Prickett know that. I'm sure they've made more than a few, themselves."

Her words didn't seem to help much. She could still see bitter self-recrimination in his expression. "It was such a stupid thing to do. Any moron should have known to apply pressure. They probably all think I'm an idiot."

"They don't think you're an idiot."

"I am an idiot. Damn it."

He was taking this relatively minor setback much harder than he should. Haley knew Ron had a streak of insecurity hiding behind his wisecracks and devil-may-care attitude. It had made an appearance during an outburst in the study group when he'd accused himself of holding the others back, implying that they'd all been carrying him through the first two years of classes and exams. He'd even offered to leave the group if they'd thought he wasn't up to their level, to everyone's shock.

They'd firmly assured him that he was as valuable a member of the group as any of them, and that not one of them had ever considered him a liability. Not even Haley, even though she'd occasionally complained that he didn't take his studies seriously enough and that he was too willing to accept the possibility that he could wash out before the end of medical school. She'd challenged him to be more positive, to stop playing the clown and be more serious and more determined to succeed against all odds, but she'd never even suggested he didn't belong among them.

She'd wondered ever since what lay behind that deeply buried self-doubt. From the very few remarks he'd made about his family, she strongly suspected the lack of confidence had been instilled years earlier. Setbacks like this, though more galling than significant, just seemed to reinforce his own self-doubt. What he needed more than the sympathy she'd already offered, she decided, was a metaphorical slap to rouse him from the self-pity party.

"You screwed up, Ron," she said, keeping her tone matter-of-fact. "It wasn't the first time, and it certainly won't be the last. Suck it up and get over it. You won't make that particular mistake again."

He blinked a couple of times, then frowned. "Yeah, you wouldn't be so casual about it if you'd given Dr. Cudahy and your resident a blood shower."

"I'd want to find a deep hole and climb into it," she admitted frankly. "But then I'd tell myself to keep going and do better next time. It's what I always do when I make a mistake—and I've made my share."

He nodded, his expression hard to read. She wondered if her words had really made an impression or if he was just placating her when he said, "Yeah, okay, thanks. You're right, of course."

"Ron—"

His mouth tilted into his usual cocky grin and he shrugged, cutting in with a dry laugh. "Hey, I got a good story out of it, right? Connor and James are going to love this. Hell, by the time I embellish it a little, it'll be hysterical. Wait until I tell them about the looks on Prickett's and Cudahy's faces."

She knew he would give no further insight into his feelings about the incident. She'd just happened to see him before he'd had a chance to erect his usual barriers, to hide his true emotions behind what she thought of as his jester's grin. Had she run into him a couple of hours later, she'd have heard the funny story and completely missed the distress beneath it.

It bothered her that he still felt the need to hide those feelings from her. From all his friends, she corrected herself quickly. There was no reason to think he'd be any more forth-coming with her, in particular, than with the others.

"You're sure you're okay?" she felt compelled to ask.

There was no reading the expression behind his eyes when he replied, "Oh, sure. I just need some clean clothes and a big ol' chunk of chocolate cake. Wouldn't have any on you, would you?"

She forced a little smile in return. "Not at the moment. But I'll make you one later, if you like."

"A pity cake?" He gave a short laugh and patted her cheek in a gesture that made her go from wanting to comfort him to wanting to punch him. "That's our Haley. Always there to boost the morale."

Before she could answer, he dropped his hand and moved toward the doorway. "I'd better go finish my assignments. See you tomorrow, Haley."

He was gone before she could respond.

Ron parked in the lot of Haley's apartment building Wednesday evening, then sat looking at her window for a few minutes. He was there to study for the shelf exams they would take at the end of their medicine rotation. They'd invited Hardik to join them. He'd agreed, but he'd said he might be running a little late and urged them to start without him.

It annoyed Ron that he was oddly hesitant to be alone with Haley until Hardik arrived.

A few days earlier, he'd been irritated with Haley for letting her matchmaking patient's teasing put awkwardness between them. Now he was the one feeling awkward because he'd let her see his chagrin at the careless mistake he'd made in front of his resident and attending.

They hadn't discussed the incident since, though there had been some ribbing from his resident during rounds Tuesday morning. Haley had not joined in the teasing, and she'd been quick to change the subject as soon as she was able. She'd considered herself rescuing him, he supposed.

He shouldn't be so perturbed that Haley knew about his gaffe. As she'd reminded him, they all did something wrong at some point in their training. Not that he'd heard of her doing anything as stupid as he had that afternoon. What galled him the most was that she'd seen him before he'd had a chance to hide his embarrassment and resulting self-doubt.

Telling himself he would just laugh it off if she brought it up this evening, turning the whole incident into a self-directed joke as he always did, he exited his vehicle. She probably wouldn't even mention it, unless she felt compelled to give him another bracing pep talk.

As he walked toward her door, he found himself hoping she'd made that chocolate pity cake. He wouldn't turn down chocolate, no matter what the motive behind the offering.

Already wearing his usual practiced grin, he rang her doorbell. The grin faded when he saw her face. She was smiling, and her makeup looked freshly applied—neither of which deceived him. He knew her too well. "What's wrong?"

"Nothing. Come on in, I made that cake I promised you."

Even cake couldn't distract him from this. "You've been crying. What happened?"

She sighed. "I didn't think you would be able to tell."

He closed the door behind him without ever taking his gaze from her face. "I can tell. What's wrong?"

If she told him this was a personal problem and none of his business, he supposed he would have to let it go. But he wanted her to know he was here for her if she needed a shoulder.

He saw her throat work with a swallow and sensed her internal debate. And then she sighed and shrugged. "Kylie Anderson called me a few minutes ago. Mr. Eddington went into cardiac arrest and died suddenly this afternoon. Half an hour after I left the hospital."

Ron grimaced. "I'm sorry, Haley. I know he was one of your favorites."

She blinked rapidly. "Yes. He was a sweet guy. Always smiling and teasing. Though he knew he didn't have long, he was hoping to go home in the next few days to spend a little more time with his family."

He rested a hand on her shoulder. "I'm sorry. But don't forget the burn-out lectures we've heard. You have to leave it at the hospital. You can't bring it home with you."

She shook her head. "I know. And I'm not going to let it affect my work. It's just sad, that's all."

Ron had always believed Haley would be an excellent physician. His only concern had been that she would take it all too personally. Get too involved with her patients, fret about the ones who wouldn't take care of themselves, and grieve over the ones who lost their ultimate fights. That was just Haley's personality—all heart. And hearts, he had learned long ago, were too easily broken.

"So you're okay?"

She smiled. "I am. Thanks for asking."

Not entirely convinced, he shook his head. "You are going to have to guard against burnout, you know. You care too much."

Her left eyebrow rose slightly. "I happen to think a doctor should care about her patients."

"There's caring. And then there's caring too much."

"Okay, I get your message. Now how about some cake?"

At least she didn't look so sad anymore, he decided before letting her sidetrack him. "Chocolate?"

The look she gave him was wry. "Would I make you any other kind?"

Laughing, he tapped her chin with his knuckles. "What a pal."

She moved quickly toward the kitchen. Had he caught just a glimpse of a flush on her cheeks before she'd turned away—

and if so, how had he embarrassed her this time? By catching her at a weak moment? Seemed like that was only fair, since she'd seen him in a few.

After only a momentary hesitation, he followed her into the small kitchen, reaching into his pocket as he walked. Haley was already slicing into a thickly frosted, dark chocolate cake that made his mouth water just to look at it. The scent of freshly brewed coffee filled the air, mingling with the chocolate aroma. Though he'd eaten dinner earlier, he was suddenly hungry again.

"That looks really good."

She smiled and set a plate holding a good-sized slice of cake on the table. "Coffee or milk?"

"Milk now. Coffee later."

She nodded and started to turn toward the fridge. He stopped her by catching her arm with his left hand. "Haley. I brought you something."

Her eyebrows rose when she looked up at him. "What did you bring?"

Feeling a little foolish, he held his right hand out to her. A bracelet of polished pink stones strung on elastic cording and tied with a jaunty little bow lay on his palm. "I know it's not like the one you broke, but I saw it in the hospital gift shop and I thought of you."

She blinked a couple of times, her long lashes sweeping down to hide the expression in her eyes. "You bought me a bracelet?"

Resisting the urge to scuff his toe on her floor like an embarrassed schoolboy, he shrugged. "I was buying a candy bar—needed my afternoon sugar fix, you know—and I saw it displayed on the counter. It wasn't all that expensive, but I thought it was kind of nice. The hospital auxiliary always needs money and you broke your bracelet and you've been helping me study, so… Anyway, it won't hurt my feelings if you don't like it."

She plucked the bauble from his hand with a smile that wavered a bit. "I like it very much. Thank you, Ron."

"I don't know what the stones are, or what they mean or anything like that. Don't know if they'll ground you or bring you wisdom or whatever. I just thought they were kind of pretty."

"I think so, too." She slipped the bracelet on her wrist and twisted her hand to admire it there. "Very pretty. Thanks again. I'll get your milk."

The doorbell rang. Ron started a little, then laughed at himself as he shook his head. "That'll be Hardik. Guess he got away earlier than he expected. I'll let him in. You'd better cut another big piece of cake."

"I'll do that."

The stones were pink opal. A stone of peace and tranquility. A healing stone.

A stone of love.

Ron wouldn't have known any of that, of course, Haley mused as she pulled the bracelet lightly between her fingers later that evening. He'd bought the bracelet because he'd thought it was pretty. Because he'd thought she might like it.

Because she had broken the one Kris gave her.

She set the bauble on her dresser and pulled a pair of silky pajamas from the top drawer. She and Hardik and Ron had put in a solid three hours of studying. Worthwhile, but draining.

Closing the drawer, she touched the bracelet again before turning away to get ready for bed.

Haley was glad to move on to the outpatient diagnostic clinic at the end of the month. She had a new resident, a new attending and new duties. Every morning she was assigned one patient for whom she conducted a full history and physical. Her resident then did a more focused physical based on the patient's complaints, and then created a treatment plan.

After the first two weeks in the clinic, she had grown somewhat more comfortable with the H & Ps. She was even getting a little faster at conducting them, to the relief, she was sure, of her patients. She didn't talk a lot about that part of her training to her mother, who wanted to hear all about Haley's days, but perhaps wouldn't have been comfortable picturing her daughter doing prostate exams on men.

Haley was still strongly considering psychiatry as an eventual specialty, but she was keeping an open mind during the rotations. She didn't have to decide for certain until early in her fourth year, when she would start applying and interviewing for residency positions. She found several areas of medicine intriguing, but psychiatry seemed to be drawing her, though she had yet to participate in actual psych practice. That would come next semester.

She still saw Ron almost every day. He was also assigned to the diagnostic clinic, though he had a different resident and attending physician for these four weeks. They passed in the hallways, and walked each other out to their cars in the afternoons. They exchanged stories about their days, and lingered in the parking lot sharing information they had learned.

She found herself looking forward to those brief, but pleasant encounters and increasingly reluctant to go her own way afterward. A few times she almost asked if he'd like to have dinner with her, but something held her back. There were a couple of times she thought Ron might have done the same thing—almost asked, but changed his mind. Which was silly, she told herself impatiently, driving home after one such awkward parting. Were they really still letting the passing comments of a former patient interfere with their friendship?

She made a vow right then that she would invite him to dinner very soon. Just a casual, friendly gesture, of course.

Maybe they'd ask Hardik if he wanted to join them. They could catch up, swap stories, compare notes over noodles or pizza.

Her phone rang just as she stepped inside her apartment. Her first thought was that it could be Ron, and it annoyed her that her pulse tripped a little at the possibility.

It was Anne's voice that greeted her when she answered the call. "Please tell me you haven't already eaten."

Haley smiled. "No, I was just trying to decide if I'm in the mood to cook tonight."

"You aren't. You really want to meet me for Mexican food."

"Craving Mexican, are you?"

"Craving a quiet hour or two with my friend."

"Surgery rotation is tough, huh?"

"That is an understatement. With my family background, I thought I was prepared. But, wow!"

Haley laughed. "Great. Now I'll be dreading that rotation after peds. At least you've got internal medicine next. That's not such a tough one."

"It's not that I don't enjoy surgery," Anne said carefully. "It's just that the hours are so long, I feel like I never get to see anyone outside of the hospital. Especially since Liam's off on another adventure in Australia. I need a couple of hours to totally forget about medicine."

"So you call another med student?"

"Who also needs a couple of hours away from the job."

"You've got that right. Give me half an hour to change and I'll meet you there."

Neither of them had to specify the place. They shared a favorite Mexican place where they met whenever they had a chance. That was one of the advantages of being such good friends, Haley thought as she went into the bedroom to freshen up and change into jeans and a cool pullover for this hot August evening. They could leave so much unsaid and still be perfectly in sync.

Which, she discovered a while later, could also be a disadvantage.

"What's going on with you, Haley?" Anne asked, studying her intently over enchiladas and *chili rellenos*.

Haley lifted both her eyebrows in an expression of confusion. "What do you mean?"

"I don't know. You just seem a little distracted this evening. Is everything going okay on your rotation?"

"Everything's fine. And I thought we agreed not to talk about work tonight, anyway."

"You know I'm always available to talk if you need to. About anything."

Haley had grown so close to Anne during the past two years. She considered Anne her closest friend, a friendship she hoped would endure long past graduation from medical school. She still had friends from high school and college, but it was hard to stay in contact with them when they were all so busy pursuing separate lives and careers. Anne shared the experience of those first two years of med school, which gave them a common base most people wouldn't quite understand.

Haley had been there for Anne when Anne had been trying to figure out how to break it to her family that she had eloped with a man her parents had strongly disapproved of. Fortunately, Anne's parents had come around to accept her husband into the family, but Anne still expressed gratitude that she'd had Haley to confide in during that stressful time. And Haley knew Anne was willing to return the favor at any time.

"Thanks, Anne. But everything's fine. Diagnostic clinic is interesting, something different every day. And I'm finally getting faster at the H & Ps, which is making my resident happy."

"That's good. How's Ron doing?"

Swallowing a sip of fruit punch a little too hard, Haley dabbed at her lips with her napkin before replying. "He's doing well. Still trying to pick up speed on his exams. You know how bad he is to get to talking with his patients and lose track of time. The patients love him, though."

"Of course. Everyone loves Ron."

"Well, not everyone." They were both aware of a few class-mates who didn't care for Ron's quirky sense of humor, and one particularly stuffy professor who'd accused Ron of not taking his training seriously enough. It was an accusation Haley had made herself a few times, before she'd figured out that Ron took his education more seriously than he allowed most others to see. So many insecurities were hidden behind that charming joker's grin of his. She still wondered what in his past had caused him to be so self-doubting, despite his usual air of easy confidence.

"Okay, most people love Ron," Anne corrected with a chuckle. "He really is a great guy."

"Yes, he is." Haley reached again for her punch glass.

"Pretty bracelet. Is it new?"

Haley glanced at the polished pink stones encircling her right wrist. "Um, yes, it is."

"I like it. I haven't seen you wear the hematite bracelet lately."

"I broke it a few weeks ago. Haven't had time to restring it yet." After a momentary hesitation, she added, "Ron gave me this one."

Anne looked noticeably unsurprised. "Did he?"

"Yeah. He was with me when I broke my other one, and he said he saw this in the hospital gift shop and bought it on impulse."

"That was nice of him." Both Anne's voice and expression were bland as she dipped a chip into salsa, giving no clue to her thoughts.

"He just bought it on a whim. He wanted to do something nice for the auxiliary and to thank me for helping him study."

"Hmm." Anne crunched the chip.

"Okay, what's that supposed to mean?"

After washing the chip down with a sip of punch, Anne replied, "I don't know what you mean. I just said, hmm."

Haley grimaced. "Sorry. Guess I'm a little oversensitive."

"Any particular reason?"

"No, it's just—" She stopped herself with a sigh. This was Anne, she reminded herself. Her best friend. "Okay, it's silly, but things have been a little…strained between Ron and me for the past few weeks."

Anne groaned. "You're fighting again?"

"No, it's not like that." Taking a deep breath, she told her friend about the awkward encounters with Ms. McMillan, leaving out the patient's name, of course. "It's so ridiculous," she concluded. "Usually Ron and I would have laughed about something like that. I don't know why we let it freak us out this time. He said it was my fault."

"Of course he did."

Haley nodded vigorously. "He always blames me."

"Mmm-hmm."

Setting down her fork, Haley frowned across the table. "You're being very cryptic tonight."

"Am I?" Anne chuckled at her own cleverness.

"Cute." Haley toyed with the pink stone bracelet for a moment before asking, "You don't think there was any truth in what my patient said, do you? I mean, about Ron…well, having feelings for me."

Her eyes soft, Anne replied, "I can't really answer that. But I think the more immediate question is—do you have feelings for Ron?"

Haley pushed her half-empty plate away, her appetite suddenly gone. "I consider Ron one of my closest friends, of course."

Even she heard the hollowness of that assertion.

"So do I," Anne said, searching Haley's face. "But I'm not getting all flustered at the thought of him, either. Liam's the only man who's ever made me feel that way."

Because Anne was head over heels in love with Liam, and claimed to have felt that way from the first time she'd met him, Haley squirmed a little in her seat in response to the comparison. "I'm not all flustered."

"Hmm." Anne scooped up a forkful of guacamole, smiling enigmatically as she ate it, and using the bite as an excuse not to say more.

Feeling her cheeks warm, Haley insisted, "I'm not flustered."

She reached jerkily for her punch glass, then swore beneath her breath when she almost dumped the red beverage in her lap. Steadying the glass quickly, she left it on the table and knotted her napkin in her nap, wondering exactly what her friend had seen in her face when she'd studied her so closely.

Did Anne know her well enough to see things Haley had been trying to hide even from herself?

Maybe she wouldn't ask Ron to dinner for a while, after all. Just until this silly phase was behind them.

Chapter Four

Ron wished he understood exactly what had changed between himself and Haley as broiling August sizzled into the first week of September. Their internal medicine rotation had ended, and the shelf exam was behind them. Haley, Ron and Hardik had met a couple more times to study for that final exam before moving on to their next rotation, pediatrics. They'd fallen easily into their customary study routines, and he was sure the reviews had helped him do well on the test.

Haley had been her usual self during those sessions. Smiling, encouraging, focused. Pushing both him and Hardik to do their best, just as she would do, herself. She laughed at their jokes, swapped stories about anonymous patients and not-so-anonymous classmates and coworkers. When he teased her, she punched his arm just as she always did, eliciting his habitual exaggerated grimace and protest.

Yet, something was different.

He couldn't help wondering if she was seeing someone again. She'd acted just this distracted when she'd first starting seeing Kris earlier that year, keeping her relationship with him quiet until Anne had accidentally mentioned it at a study session where she'd been overheard.

He'd disliked Kris from the beginning. Couldn't put his finger on the reason, exactly; the guy seemed pleasant enough. Just…bland. Way too docile and colorless for Haley. Besides which, it had been a terrible time to get involved with anyone. Second year was a nightmare of classes, tests and preparation for Step 1; it was a crazy time to start a new romance. He'd worried about her being distracted, falling behind, doing something she would regret.

He should have known better, of course. Haley would let nothing interfere with her set path. She'd entertained herself with Kris for a time, then cheerfully moved on, neither the worse for wear.

Ron had dated during that year, himself. Occasionally. Very casually.

No one had even tempted him to enter a relationship.

Was Haley seeing someone new now that third year had brought a little more spare time? Was she seeing Kris again?

Not that he could blame Kris if he was trying to get her back. Spotting Haley across the hospital parking lot as he walked toward his car, he pushed his hands into the pockets of his gray dress pants. She did look good in the leaf green top and taupe skirt, and the shoes she wore made her legs look a mile long and nicely curvy. But then, Haley always looked good. Fresh, pretty, appealing.

He tried not to think of her that way. Like he'd told her, he would never want to risk messing up their friendship. It meant too much to him. But he wasn't blind, and he wasn't a eunuch. He was keenly aware that his friend was seriously hot.

"Hey, Haley!" he called out on impulse, speeding his steps.

She looked over her shoulder with a smile, pausing at the driver's door of her car. "Hi, Ron."

"Got plans for this evening?"

"No, why?"

"How about a baseball game?"

She blinked. "A baseball game?"

Resisting the impulse to tease her about the echo, he nodded casually. "Dr. Beck gave me two box-seat tickets for the Travs game tonight. It might be fun to get away from work for a few hours. What do you say?"

"You want me to go with you to the Travelers' game?"

Laughing, he waved a hand in front of her eyes. "Hello? Anyone home? Why do you keep repeating me?"

Shaking her head a little, Haley gave him a self-conscious smile. "Sorry. I guess my brain's a little fried from a very busy day."

"Then you could definitely use a night off. What do you say? Popcorn? Peanuts? Cotton candy?"

She hesitated just long enough to make him wonder if she was trying to come up with an excuse to decline. He held his breath, hoping she'd say yes. It was no big deal, after all. Just two friends spending an evening together. Two very good friends.

And then she lifted her chin and shrugged. "Sure. Why not? I haven't been to a baseball game in years."

Satisfaction flooded through him. "Great. It'll be fun. Maybe you'll even catch a foul ball."

"I'd be more likely to get hit in the head by one."

He grinned. "I'll pick you up in an hour. Don't bother eating first."

"I plan to pig out on ballpark food."

"Same here. See you."

He was pleased to see she was smiling when she slid behind the wheel of her car. She appeared as though she might even be looking forward to the outing. He knew he was.

A good-sized crowd had gathered at the North Little Rock ballpark on this pleasantly mild evening for one of the last games of the season. The redbrick exterior of the relatively new park, featuring an impressive clock tower and old-fashioned wrought-iron streetlights, was designed to resemble an old-time train station. This was Haley's first time to visit, and she was impressed by how pretty and welcoming the entrances appeared.

Ron placed a casual hand on her back as they entered one of the three gates, shoulder to shoulder with other arrivals. She knew it was just a way to keep them from getting separated, but she was keenly aware of the contact between them.

They entered into a covered concourse lined with gift shops and concession stands. Music played from overhead speakers, people milled about and talked and laughed, children dashed, squealing from one end to the other, some wearing Little League uniforms and carrying ball gloves. Scents of popcorn, cotton candy, hot dogs, barbecue and beer wafted past her nose, making her tummy rumble in response. Lunch had been a long time ago.

"Food now, snacks later?" Ron asked.

"Sounds good to me."

They debated going into the bar and grill but decided to take food to their seats, instead. Part of the fun of eating at the ballpark was risking splattering food all over their clothes, Ron asserted with a grin. Because Haley was wearing a dark red, short-sleeve pullover with comfortable, dark wash jeans and red-and-black ballet slippers, she wasn't overly worried about her clothes.

She didn't want to think about the ridiculous amount of time she had spent deciding what to wear, even though she'd had less than an hour to get ready and change before Ron picked her up after work. The scoop-neck tee had been the third shirt she'd tried on. She'd settled on it finally because it was casual enough not to look as though she'd put too much thought into her clothing choice, yet still fitted enough to flatter, something her feminine ego had demanded. Though Ron hadn't commented on her outfit, she thought she'd seen appreciation in his eyes when she'd opened her door to him.

He looked darned good, himself, in a loose-fitting, soft green Hawaiian print shirt and khaki cargo shorts with sandals. His sandy hair was tousled around his face, making him look young and sporty and appealing. Though no one would call him a "pretty boy," he looked more like an athlete or a male model than an aspiring doctor, definitely attractive enough to pose for one of those beach ads in a travel magazine. She was aware of the attention he received from young women milling around the concourse while they ordered their food.

The thing was, Ron seemed almost oblivious to his attraction, she reflected, settling into her comfortable green plastic box seat with her hot dog and bottled water. He'd made a few joking remarks about James's classically handsome face—to James's embarrassment and everyone else's amusement—but Haley had never seen an ounce of vanity in Ron, himself. He dressed casually, cared nothing about designer names, wore a practical, inexpensive watch, favored comfort over fashion in his shoes.

He'd mentioned that he'd grown up without much money, so he'd never gotten spoiled to the finer things in life, but she doubted that money would change him much. Ron just wasn't in "the game," as she thought of it—that constant striving to impress, to possess, to accumulate. She'd always admired that about him, having little interest in those things, herself.

Her own family had struggled financially when her father had been laid off from his job while she was a freshman in high school. He'd taken the opportunity to fulfill a lifelong dream and open a little Italian restaurant, and Haley had dedicated herself to helping her parents make that dream pay off, working long, unpaid hours in the restaurant after school and on holidays and for two years after her high school graduation. Her parents would never get rich with their establishment, but they had the satisfaction of making a decent living with it now and having a loyal and appreciative customer base. She was so proud of them for following their dreams, just as they had encouraged her to do.

"How's your hot dog?" Ron asked, looking up from his nachos loaded with cheese, peppers and barbecued pork.

She swallowed a bite of all-beef frank, bun and mustard and then smiled. "It's delicious. Hot dogs always taste best at a ballpark. How's your heart-attack-in-a-bowl?"

Laughing, he scooped up more melted yellow cheese onto an already-loaded tortilla chip. "It's great. I'll eat an extra helping of veggies at lunch tomorrow to make up for the indulgence."

"And I'll eat salad tomorrow," she joked in return. "Because I am definitely having cotton candy before I leave here tonight."

A blast of organ music and a stir of reaction from the crowd signaled the beginning of the minor league baseball game. The clatter of inflatable plastic "thunder sticks" blended with the cacophony of other sounds, and while it was noisy, Haley found the atmosphere oddly relaxing. Probably because it was so different from her usual routines.

It really was a beautiful early evening. Far on the other side of the park, beyond right field, children frolicked on the grassy berms and climbed on playground equipment. Families and company groups milled beneath rented picnic pavilions. She couldn't see the Arkansas River flowing on the other side of the park, but the Little Rock skyline on the far side of the river provided the backdrop for the game. Old warehouses and new skyscrapers were stacked like plastic building blocks against the darkening blue sky. Because their seats faced west, Haley was glad she'd thought to wear her sunglasses against the glare of the setting sun. Ron had slipped on a pair of aviators, but quite a few of the people surrounding them were squinting and shading their eyes with their hands, including the giggly teenage girls sitting on Haley's right.

Vendors in red-and-white striped shirts and bulging red cash aprons climbed the steps hawking peanuts, popcorn, Cracker Jacks, cotton candy and cold beer. Someone dressed as the team mascot, Shelley, a bucktoothed brown horse in a Travelers jersey and cap, worked the crowd, posing with excited children and making them laugh with his antics.

Both Haley and Ron were entertained by a little boy in the row directly in front of them. Blond and blue-eyed, he might have been two years old. He looked adorable in his tiny baseball cap and jersey, and he held a soft toddler-sized catcher's mitt that he swung enthusiastically, hitting both his indulgent parents in the head more than once. He liked to stand backward in his seat, flirting with Haley. She flirted in return, making him grin and bounce. Ron also teased the boy, eliciting musical laughs.

Ron was good with kids, Haley noted. It was no wonder he was doing so well on the peds rotation so far. He liked seniors and toddlers, he'd said. Both groups adored him.

The home team scored a home run late in the third inning, and the crowd erupted in cheers. Their hands empty now, Haley and Ron joined the celebration, standing to clap and high-five as two runners crossed home plate, bringing the score to 3–1. They laughed together at the between-inning antics on the field—mascot races, potato-sack races, dizzy-bat races. The sun went down and the park lights blazed, and she and Ron removed their dark glasses. He knew much more about the game than she did, and he patiently answered her questions about rules and strategy. There were no awkward pauses, for which she was grateful. She was simply enjoying this outing with him.

By the sixth inning, Ron decided he was ready for his next course of ballpark food. He debated between a funnel cake and a soft pretzel, while Haley flagged down a vendor and pointed to a cone of pink cotton candy. She rationalized the purchase by reminding herself that the treat was mostly air, and probably the lowest calories of the choices, despite the lack of nutritional value.

"Can I bring you something to drink?" Ron asked as he stood to go fetch his own dessert, having finally decided on the funnel cake.

"No, thanks, I still have part of my bottled water."

He nodded. "Okay, be right back. Don't run off with any hot ballplayers while I'm gone."

"Well, darn, take all the fun out of the evening, why don't you?" she joked in return.

The two teenage girls on Haley's right had giggled and ogled the ballplayers throughout the game, more interested in posing and performing than in hits and runs. The parents of one of the girls sat at the other end of the row, and had mostly ignored the teens during the game. Still, the teens hadn't been particularly annoying and Haley had been amused by their artless chattering, though she'd had no real interaction with them to that point.

Just as Ron walked away, the girl next to Haley dropped the cell phone she'd spent a significant amount of time texting on. The phone landed near Haley's foot, so she bent to scoop it up with her free hand and return it.

"Doesn't look like it was damaged," she said reassuringly.

The fresh-faced redhead clutched the phone as though it were encrusted with priceless gems. "Thank you."

"You're welcome."

"Great game, isn't it?"

Responding to the girl's earnest attempt at polite chitchat, Haley nodded with a smile. "Yes, it is."

"I think the Travs are going to win."

"I hope you're right." The home team was still ahead by two runs, but the opposing team was giving them strong competition.

The girl leaned a little closer, lowering her voice to a conspiratorial murmur barely audible above the surrounding noise. "My friend and I think your boyfriend is really cute. Is he a ballplayer?"

"He's not—" Haley stopped her automatic correction, deciding it was more trouble than it was worth. "No, he's a medical student."

The girl's eyes widened. "He's a doctor? Cool. Are you a nurse?"

"I'm also a medical student."

"Oh. Cool."

"He's really funny." The blonde on the redhead's other side leaned forward to make the comment, not wanting to be left out of the conversation. "He's been making us laugh with some of his comments about the game."

Before Haley could reply, Ron returned, carrying a funnel cake and a soda. Seeing the teens looking at him, he nodded affably. "Evening, ladies."

They dissolved into giggles.

Ron and Haley shared a quizzical look as he took his seat beside her. "Want a bite?" he asked, offering the warm, fragrant treat.

She shook her head and plucked a puff of cotton candy from the paper cone in her hand. "I'm still working on this, thanks."

He watched as she popped the candy into her mouth, letting it dissolve on her tongue. His gaze lingered for a moment on her lips, then lifted slowly to meet her eyes. "Is it good, sugar?"

She blinked. "Um—?"

"Your cotton candy," he said, all innocence. "Good sugar?"

Shaking her head a little, she replied, "Yes, it's very good. Oh, look. Why is that guy yelling at the umpire?"

Chuckling at the obvious change of subject, he obligingly talked about the game.

The seventh inning had just begun when the woman sitting in front of them started to scream. "Dylan? Dylan? Someone help me, he's choking!"

The child's father had left his seat only moments before, perhaps headed for the restrooms. The mother bent over her son in her lap, frantically patting his back. The boy was suspiciously still.

Both Ron and Haley sprang forward instinctively to help, even as the people in surrounding seats leaned forward to gawk. Her heart in her throat, Haley noted that the child's lips were already turning blue.

"Would you let me take him, ma'am?" Ron asked, leaning over the seat.

The woman looked up at him with panicky wet eyes. "Can you help?"

"They're doctors," the redheaded teenager said avidly. "Both of them," she added, waving a hand toward Ron and Haley.

"We're medical students." Ron was already reaching for the child, and Haley reached out to help him.

"What was he eating?" she asked the mother.

"I gave him a bite of my hot dog. I thought he'd chewed it up, but then he stopped breathing. Oh, my God, Dylan!"

Ron swept a finger into the boy's throat while Haley tried to calm the boy's mother. Other people were already running toward them, including a police officer and the boy's frantic father.

Haley's knees went weak with relief when the child suddenly gagged, coughed and burst into tears. "He'll be all right now," she assured the mother.

Ron handed the boy to his father. Another man approached from another box. "I'm a doctor. Is there anything I can do to help?"

Haley let Ron confer with the doctor while she continued to reassure the weeping mother that the child would be okay.

"It was just a little bite," the woman wailed, obviously berating herself.

"These things happen often," Haley assured her. "Hot dogs are one of the more dangerous foods for children because of their round shape. Fortunately, Ron was able to dislodge it fairly easily."

"I'll never let him eat a hot dog again."

Smiling a little, Haley shook her head. "Just make sure the pieces are very small while he's so young. He'll be fine."

A blast of organ music announced the seventh inning stretch. "Take Me Out to the Ball Game" played while Dylan's parents effusively thanked Ron and Haley and then carried their sleepy boy away.

"You know, we both have to be at work early in the morning," Ron murmured to Haley. "Whenever you're ready to go, I'm okay with it."

Relieved, she nodded. As much as she'd enjoyed the outing, she was getting a little tired, especially now that the adrenaline rush of the crisis was receding. Smiling a goodbye at the thoroughly impressed teenagers, she accompanied Ron toward the exit.

* * *

The quiet in Ron's car was rather a relief after the commotion at the ballpark. Haley sat back in the comfortable passenger seat of the aging sedan, drawing a deep breath and letting it out slowly.

"Tired?" he asked as he guided the car from the parking lot, merging carefully with the traffic on Broadway headed toward I-30.

"A little. I had a very good time, though. Until that child started choking, anyway. That scared the socks off me."

Ron grimaced. "I know what you mean. My hands were shaking so hard I had a tough time sweeping his throat. I can't tell you how glad I was that the food was lodged within fairly easy reach."

She half turned beneath her fastened seat belt to study his face. "You looked so calm. I was really impressed with how well you handled that. Especially since we've been on peds for such a short time."

"Thanks. It was actually my second time to stop a kid from choking that way. My sister's kid choked on a candy at a family gathering when I was in college. Everyone started screaming and yelling and pounding on his back, and I was the only one who thought to reach in and dislodge the candy."

The rare glimpse into his past intrigued her. "You've never mentioned you have a nephew."

"I've got a couple of them. Haven't seen them in a while. My sister moved to Florida a couple of years ago. She's not one to stay in touch."

"You have two brothers, don't you? Do you stay in contact with them?"

He shrugged. "One's on the carnie circuit, so I rarely see him. The other's in prison in Mississippi. Long story, and one I'm not fond of discussing."

She couldn't blame him for that. "Was that when you decided you wanted to be a doctor? When you saved your nephew?"

He hesitated only a moment before replying. "Maybe it got me thinking along those lines. That, and a science professor I was pretty close to. He thought I'd make a good doctor, and he sort of pushed me into taking the MCAT. I was so sure I'd blow it that I was as surprised as anyone when I scored high enough to actually be considered for med school."

She shook her head in response to his expressed self-doubt. "You've never given yourself enough credit. You belong in medical school as much as any of us, Ron."

He chuckled lightly. "I was just lucky that enough accepted applicants changed their mind so I got in as an alternate that year. I didn't think I'd make it in."

"Well, you did. And you've done very well. You'll make a great doctor. You proved that yet again at the ballpark tonight."

The smile he slanted her way had a wry edge to it. "I always appreciate your pep talks."

She frowned. Was he making fun of her again?

After a moment, she tried again to keep the conversation moving. "Your parents must be very proud of you."

"Hmm."

Her frown deepened. "What does that mean?"

Keeping his eyes on the road, he answered lightly, "You'd think they would be. Let's just say, my parents aren't exactly the encouraging types. My dad's always out in his auto repair shop, and when he's not he sits in his chair staring at the TV and drinking too much beer. My mom's obsessed with keeping a clean house, raising African violets and doing various handcrafts. She criticizes everything anyone else does. Nothing satisfies her. Not everyone is as lucky as you are to be so close with your parents."

She'd talked quite a bit about her family during the past two years, so Ron knew all about her happy childhood, the financial crisis during her teens, the restaurant venture of which she was so proud. He had even met her parents when the whole study group had celebrated the end of the first school year at their restaurant in Russellville. Haley had wanted to introduce her parents to all her study friends, who'd been so important to her during that first stressful year.

Though his words about his family were rather bitter, his tone had been more resigned. As if he'd long ago accepted the reality of his situation and had chosen not to dwell on it.

"Maybe you and your family will be able to repair your relationship eventually. I'm sure if you keep trying, you'll find some common ground with your parents and your siblings. And I'd bet they're more proud of you than you realize."

He flipped on his turn signal to prepare to exit the freeway toward her apartment. "Not every bad situation can be repaired, Haley. Sometimes it really is best to accept reality."

"You can't just give up on having a good relationship with your family."

He sighed gustily. "What is it with you and never giving up? There are times when that's the best choice for all involved."

She wasn't going to concede that, especially when it came to family. But she knew there was no need to argue further now. Ron would only turn it into an excuse to mock her about being an incurable cheerleader, as he always did.

In a characteristically teasing show of chivalry, he walked her to her door a short while later. "I'll protect you against any ninja bad guys who could be lurking behind the bushes," he assured her when she told him there was no need for him to accompany her.

She glanced ironically around the well-lit, neatly landscaped, comfortably harmless parking lot before looking up at him again. "And who's going to protect you?"

He put a hand to his heart and staggered comically. "*Zing.* Right to the male ego. You wound, Haley."

She punched his arm. "You are so full of it, Gibson."

He laughed and rubbed the spot she'd barely tapped. "I'm going to have permanent scars from all those punches by the time I graduate—if I ever do, of course."

Was he trying to taunt her into another "cheerleader" speech? If so, she resisted, merely giving him a look when she stuck her key into her door. "Good. You'll have something to remember me by."

He reached out to brush a strand of hair off her cheek. "I won't need scars to help me remember you, Haley."

His fingertips lingered for a moment against her suddenly warm skin. Her hand going still on the doorknob, she gazed up at him, trying to recover enough breath to bid him a casual good night.

What breath remained escaped in a soft whoosh when he ran his thumb across her lower lip, a slow, undeniably seductive gesture that made her fingers tighten convulsively on the doorknob. To stop them from reaching for him, perhaps?

His gaze on her mouth, he murmured, "You know, if this had been a date, I'd be making a move to kiss you good-night right now."

She managed to speak with some semblance of her usual voice. "Then I guess it's a good thing it wasn't a date, huh?"

His eyes lifting to hers, he asked, "And if it had been? Would you be making a smooth move to evade that kiss?"

She couldn't help glancing at his upturned lips. Imagining them pressed to hers. Silently, she cleared her throat before attempting a jokingly flirtatious smile. "That's for me to know."

His left eyebrow quirked as if in recognition of a challenge. But he merely stroked his thumb across her lip again, then dropped his hand and turned away. "I'll see you at work tomorrow, Haley. Thanks for going to the ball game with me."

She slipped inside her door and closed it behind her before leaning back against the wood with a long, shaky exhale.

If Ron *had* tried to kiss her?

Something told her that she wouldn't have tried to evade him at all.

Which meant she probably wouldn't be sleeping much tonight. She'd be lying awake wondering when her feelings for Ron had undergone such a transformation—or had she been this intrigued by him all along without admitting it even to herself?

Chapter Five

The class tailgate party was held on the third Saturday in September. Haley and the other officers had worked hard putting it together; maybe she'd worked just a little harder than the others, she acknowledged privately, but she hadn't really minded the extra duties. She thought it would be fun to have the whole class together again after they'd been separated in rotations for almost three months now, half the class on one semester schedule, the remaining half on the other.

She didn't want to admit she'd deliberately stayed so busy to avoid spending time with anyone in particular—or to put off analyzing her feelings about that particular someone.

The class had reserved a grassy area outside the stadium, where they'd set up an awning. Charcoal grills donated by class members were already smoking, the fragrant aromas of charcoal and roasting meat mingling with the scents of beer and lingering summer heat. Wearing jeans and the requisite red-and-white shirt of the home football team, Haley had arrived early, zipping from spot to spot to make sure the tables were ready for the potluck dishes steadily arriving, that the disposable plates and utensils and napkins were conveniently arranged, that the red-and-white decorations fluttered invitingly from every available surface.

Other tailgate parties were going on all through the parking lot and spilling onto the golf course that abutted the stadium. A red-and-white circus was taking place around them; at this point, the upcoming game was only a secondary consideration to the fun. The med-school class had staked out a good-sized patch of grass for their festivities, and already it was filling with classmates in lawn chairs and children dashing frantically underfoot.

As more people arrived, she had help with her chores. Connor brought Mia and his daughter, Alexis, each bearing plates of food to contribute. Alexis was soon romping with the other kids, playing with the Frisbees and foam footballs and other toys that had been provided for them. At eight, she was older than most of the other classmates' children, but she seemed happy to play patiently with the littler ones, who adored having the attention of a "big kid."

Visibly pleased that Liam was in town to join them, Anne accompanied her husband from the parking lot. She carried a potluck dish; Liam bore a couple of stadium cushions for the game that followed. James arrived soon afterward, bringing cookies probably made by his housekeeper. The study group was fully represented when Ron arrived just barely on time, ruefully contributing bakery brownies to the spread.

Haley was delighted with the turnout. Almost two-thirds of the class had shown up, which was a very good showing compared to some past events. Considering that there were quite a few who weren't able to get away from their hospital chores, and a few others who just weren't interested in socializing with their classmates, it was a great success.

She'd already been by the hospital that morning and gotten her responsibilities out of the way, so she was able to concentrate on her class officer duties. She mingled among the crowd, chatting, catching up, finding out how everyone was doing in their rotations. It was especially nice to see the ones on the opposite semester schedule. She ran into the ones on her semester schedule during lectures, but rarely crossed paths with the other classmates anymore, and she missed them. She'd spent two years sitting for hours a day in the same classroom with all these people, and that experience created a bond even among the ones who didn't know each other well.

Stacks of food were consumed; beer, water and soft drinks downed thirstily. Adults laughed and chattered and mingled; children played and squealed and cried. One little boy fell and scraped his knees. Fifty aspiring doctors gathered to proclaim him okay, to Haley's amusement.

An impromptu game of touch football for the adults began after everyone had eaten all they could hold. They were somewhat limited in the grassy area provided for them, but they made the most of the space they had. Only twenty or so were interested in playing; the others gathered around to corral the children and cheer on the players.

Joining the group preparing to play, Haley noticed that "Margo the Magnificent," as she and Anne had dubbed their class president, was staying far away from the playing field. Margo was as immaculately dressed as always, not a bleached hair out of place, as she moved through the crowd accepting accolades for how well the event had turned out. Though Haley was well aware Margo had done little more than assign responsibilities to others in the class, she didn't resent the attention the other woman received. Margo really was an exceptional student; delegation was just one of Margo's many talents, she thought with a wry smile.

The study group made sure they were on the same team, though Anne was content to stay on the bench most of the time. Mia and Alexis stood on the sidelines, clapping and cheering when Connor—the former high school coach— made impressive plays. It got pretty silly—partially because everyone was enjoying a rare day of play and relaxation and partially due to the beer that had flowed so freely that afternoon. Haley hadn't laughed so much in a long time.

At one point, she found the ball in her hands. While she wondered how she'd ended up with it, her teammates screamed at her to run for the makeshift goal line. She ran. Her teammates surrounded her, blocking the other team's attempts to stop her. Giggling, she evaded an outstretched hand. Ron threw himself on the ground behind her, tripping anyone who tried to get past him.

"Go, Haley! Save yourself!" he shouted dramatically.

Laughing, she crossed the goal line.

Since no one had actually been keeping score, she had no idea if her touchdown put their team ahead, but they celebrated, anyway.

"Let's see your TD dance," Ron ordered, brushing grass from his red shirt as he ran toward her.

Grinning, she wiggled her hips a little.

Ron blew a raspberry in disgust. "That's not a victory dance. *This* is a victory dance."

Swinging his arms wildly, he mimicked a pro football player's touchdown celebration, adding a few flourishes of his own. After tossing the football to someone else, she punched Ron's arm. "You are such a ham."

He threw the oft-abused arm loosely around her shoulders, giving her a hug that might have been almost brotherly, except for the way it made her heart race. Her face was flushed when he dropped his arm and turned to answer something Connor said. She hoped everyone would blame that on the exertion of the game.

Turning toward the drinks table, she found herself face-to-face with Anne, who was studying her much too closely for comfort.

She glanced around at her other friends and classmates, wondering how many were speculating about whatever might be developing between her and Ron. Or was she only imagining that anyone thought about them at all?

This was getting much too complicated. And if she had any sense at all, she'd put a stop to it now, before she and Ron strayed any deeper into dangerous waters. But something told her she was already caught in a current that she wouldn't escape completely unscathed.

She busied herself with clearing away the remains of the party, trying to push any musings about Ron to the back of her mind for now. But like the man, himself, her thoughts of him had a way of grabbing and holding her full attention.

Ron knew by his second week on the children's hematology and oncology ward that he'd found his medical calling. He was fascinated by the practice, though he didn't immediately tell anyone he wanted to continue in it. More than a few people would be surprised if he expressed an interest in that specialty, he theorized as he sat in a hospital coffee shop late Thursday afternoon, nursing a cappuccino and biscotti and contemplating his future. Pedi hem-onc was a challenging and competitive specialty, requiring a great deal of dedication, meticulous attention to detail, and total commitment—none of which he was known for to this point.

Yet still he could see himself in the practice. He liked the fact that the hem-onc doctors developed one-on-one relationships with their patients. That they had so much interaction with the families. That they had the opportunity to provide futures for children diagnosed with potentially devastating diseases.

The children's suffering and their parents' anguish were heart wrenching. He'd already lost one brave little patient; a sweet-faced little girl had quietly slipped away Monday afternoon while her parents, the attending, the resident and Ron had been present. He'd thought of Haley's grief over her Mr. Eddington as he'd fought tears of his own in the solitude of his apartment that evening. You couldn't take it home with you—but as she'd said, it would require a heart of stone not to be affected by the human tragedies physicians dealt with on a daily basis. He never wanted to get to a point where such a sad loss didn't disturb him at all.

Still, for every loss there were many success stories. Children who left the hospital with long, healthy futures ahead of them, thanks to rapidly developing advances in modern medicine. Teenagers who would attend their proms, attain their driver's licenses, fall in love and have children of their own.

He wanted to be a part of that field. And yet he still had to get through more rotations, more shelf exams, the two-part, second step of the national licensure exam, residency applications and interviews, the uncertain wait to be accepted into one of those exclusive residency programs. So many pitfalls ahead of him, any of which could derail his dreams.

He knew how Haley would respond if he said something along that line to her. She'd go directly into cheerleader mode, assuring him that he could succeed at anything, bolstering his ego with pithy pep talks and cheery platitudes. She'd mean every word of it, of course; optimism was as much a part of Haley's true nature as cynicism was of his. If she had any doubts about his suitability for that specialty—and he suspected she would—she would keep them well hidden.

As if he'd subconsciously called her to him by thinking of her, she walked into the coffee shop, pausing only a moment when she saw him sitting alone at a tiny table for two. She ordered a coffee and a fruit-and-yogurt cup, then carried them over to join him.

Because she was on the pulmonology ward while he worked hem-onc, they had seen each other only in passing during the ten days that had passed since the tailgate party. Even those few days apart had made him miss her. He savored the sight of her in her blue top and dark pants beneath the white coat she kept so snowy white and immaculately pressed. A navy band held her tidy bob in place, keeping her hair out of her lightly made-up face. Haley didn't fuss with her appearance the way Margo and some of the others did, but she always looked fresh and pretty. Ron much preferred that particular look.

Automatically, he smoothed a hand over his own clean but slightly rumpled white coat and wrinkled khaki slacks when she walked toward him.

"How's it going?" she asked as she slipped into the tiny, round-seated metal chair on the other side of the table.

"Not bad. You?"

She smiled. "Same. I missed lunch today. I needed a snack to get me through the rest of the afternoon."

"I had a quick lunch, but I'm killing half an hour while I wait for a meeting with my resident."

Dipping a plastic spoon into her yogurt, Haley laughed softly. "We always seem to be eating something when we're together."

He leaned back in his chair and grinned. "That's the med student's life. Long hours, little sleep and grab-food-when-you-get-the-chance."

"I guess that's true. At least this year's not nearly as bad as last year. Though Anne warned me the surgery rotation is exhausting."

"James said the same about ob-gyn. He's definitely not going into that field."

"Has he decided yet what he does want to do?"

"Not as far as he's mentioned. You're still set on psychiatry?"

"At the moment. Still liking peds now that you're actually seeing it first hand?"

"Very much." He wouldn't mention just then that he was flirting with the idea of a hem-onc specialty. She probably figured he was considering general pediatrics.

She nodded. "That doesn't surprise me. You're so good with kids. You'll be a wonderful pediatrician, if that's what you decide to pursue."

Two minutes into their conversation, he thought with a smothered smile. It never took her long to work in a pep talk. Though there had been a time when he'd been irked by her relentless encouragement—when he'd been at his lowest in self-confidence—he found it rather endearing now. But he could say that about most of Haley's little quirks.

He was gradually arriving at the realization that the ailing Ms. McMillan had been a very wise woman.

"I've barely seen you since the tailgate party," he commented.

"I know. With the hours we put in here and being on call occasionally and studying for each day's lecture, there just hasn't been much free time."

"The tailgate party was a big success. Everyone's talked about how much fun they had. You did a great job."

She beamed in pleasure at the compliment. "Thanks. I thought it went well. We're working on planning the Halloween party now. I hope that goes as well."

The annual Halloween party was always a success. A joint venture between the schools of medicine and law, it involved lots of wild costumes and free-flowing beverages. Ron had skipped out his freshman year in favor of studying with all the group except Connor, who'd taken Alexis trick-or-treating that night, but Ron had attended last year's bash. Dressed as a jar of cotton swabs—which had involved many cotton balls stuck in his hair and an aluminum "lid" for a topping—he'd had a good time. The only downside had been watching Haley attend with a date.

It hadn't been Kris; that had been a few months before she'd started dating him. She'd attended the party with a law student who lived in the same apartment complex as her. Though it was obvious that there was nothing serious going on between them, Ron still hadn't been particularly pleased to watch her dancing with the other man, and that had been before he'd acknowledged even to himself that he had special feelings for Haley. She'd looked so darned pretty in a Cleopatra costume that had revealed intriguing slices of creamy skin—not too much, but enough to get his imagination going. Her companion had been decked out as Julius Caesar. Ron hadn't cared for the guy, though he hadn't disliked him as much as he had Kris.

Because he didn't want to go through that again, he said on impulse, "Maybe you and I could go to the Halloween bash together? I know it's almost six weeks away, but we could use the time to come up with some fun costume ideas."

Her long lashes swept downward, hiding her eyes as she toyed with her snack. "Like you said, it's six weeks away. It sort of depends on what our schedules are like then. One or both of us could end up on call."

Frowning, he asked himself if that was a brush-off. A way for her to let him know she wasn't interested in attending the party with him.

He felt ridiculously like a smitten schoolboy, trying to read her expression, trying to keep his cool—and his ego—intact while still angling for a date with her. He couldn't say he cared for being in that situation at his age.

"Yeah," he said, trying not to speak too curtly. "It all depends, of course."

She raised her gaze to his face, and the anxious look in her eyes told him that she worried she'd hurt his feelings. "Don't get me wrong, I'd be happy to go to the party with you if our schedules allow. It sounds like fun. Maybe the whole gang can get together that night. Anne and Liam and James and whoever he wants to bring, if anyone. Maybe Connor and Mia can join us after they take Alexis trick-or-treating. Our party usually starts after kids are in bed."

"The whole gang. Sure. That would be great. It's always good when we can get together these days."

"Um, Ron?"

He crumpled the plastic wrapping from his biscotti and stood to toss it in a nearby trash can. "Guess I'd better get back to the ward. My resident should be available soon."

She reached out to catch his arm when he passed her. "Ron, wait."

He paused. "Yeah?"

"How about dinner tonight?"

The blurted question took him by surprise. "Um— dinner?"

"Yes." She nodded firmly, as if to convince both of them. "We can meet somewhere...or you could come to my place. I'll cook, if you like. I made and froze a lasagna a couple weeks ago. It wouldn't take long to thaw out and warm it up for dinner."

He searched her face, wondering if this was another pity gesture. A concession to his pride? An implicit apology for the brush-off of the Halloween invitation? He didn't like any of those possibilities. And yet...

"Sure," he said lightly. "I'll bring the wine."

"That sounds good. I'll see you at about seven, then."

Nodding, he took a step backward, making his escape before she had a chance to change her mind. "See you, Haley."

"Yeah." Her tone was just a bit hesitant, as if she was already wondering if this was a mistake. "See you tonight, Ron."

She considered calling Hardik or James. Either or both of the bachelors would probably have enjoyed a home-cooked meal. She was sure Ron would enjoy spending a casual evening chatting with them.

She was equally sure that he would think she'd invited them because she'd been a coward. Afraid to be alone with him.

He'd have been right.

It wasn't that she was afraid of Ron. She trusted him implicitly. She was the one who'd been acting strangely lately. Whose impulses seemed to be getting out of hand. Like this dinner invitation, for example. What had made her invite him to her place for a cozy, meal à deux?

Though she'd tried all afternoon to rationalize the invitation by telling herself that it had been a gesture to apologize for her inadvertently rude response to his Halloween party suggestion, she knew that wasn't quite the whole story. The thing was, it was getting harder to deny her attraction to Ron—and his to her. It was time for them to either do something about it, clear the air, or allow their friendship to be irreparably damaged—something she wasn't willing to risk.

He arrived exactly on time, bearing the bottle of wine he'd promised. Knowing her behavior was a bit too animated, she served dinner immediately, chattering and laughing the whole time. Ron played along, teasing and joking as he always did, though something in his eyes let her know he was as aware as her of the underlying tension between them now.

The chocolate torte she'd thrown together for dessert was a big hit, as anything chocolate always was where Ron was concerned. They continued to talk shop while they finished the meal. Ron shared stories about the hem-onc ward, and Haley told him about the children she worked with in pulmonology. One cystic fibrosis patient had particularly captured her heart, a six-year-old boy who'd been hospitalized with pneumonia, but was making a satisfactory recovery. Even with his health ailments, the child was sunny-natured and funny, wrapping the entire hospital staff around his little fingers.

"Sounds like you rather enjoy peds, yourself," Ron commented as he helped her stack dishes after the meal.

"I do like it. I'm thinking maybe I'll specialize in child psych, rather than adult."

"You could do a double board residency. Get certified in both."

"Actually, I've been looking into the triple board program," she confessed. "Child and adult psych and peds. It's a five-year program, but I'd be board certified in all three, which would really open my options for the future."

He didn't look particularly surprised by her aspiration. "I see. So you'll definitely be leaving the state for your residency, since there's not a triple board program here."

"Yes, I would have to go somewhere else if I decide to go that route. But I plan to come back to Arkansas eventually. My roots are here."

"Hmm."

She wasn't sure how to interpret that murmur. "Are you hoping to get into the peds residency here?"

He shrugged. "You never know. All depends on passing Step 2. And getting through the interview process."

She gave him a look as she turned from the dishwasher. "You're not preparing for failure, are you?"

He grinned. "Sugar, I'm always prepared for failure. Better to expect it and be pleasantly surprised than hope for the best and be blindsided."

She sighed, hiding her reaction to his contagious smile behind exasperation. "You know how I disapprove of that attitude."

"Yes, I know." Taking a step toward her, he blocked her path, effectively trapping her against the kitchen counter. He lifted a hand to stroke a strand of hair from her cheek, letting his fingertips linger against her skin. He'd done that once before. It was no less disconcerting this time. "You've disapproved of me from the day you met me, haven't you, Haley?"

"I, um—" She moistened her lips. "Of course not, Ron. We struck up a conversation the day we met, remember?"

"I remember. I mentioned my Plan B—being a mortician—and you gave me a locker-room talk about giving it my best and winning for the home team."

"I didn't say anything about the home team," she muttered with a frown. "And I didn't disapprove of you. You're the one who had a problem with my attitude. You called me a cheerleader."

"Mmm. As in motivator. Inspirer. Encourager. None of which are bad things."

She couldn't tell if he was mocking her or complimenting her. Maybe a little of both. She did notice that he wasn't backing away. In fact, she thought he might have inched a little closer.

"Ron?"

His gaze lingered on her mouth. "I've been thinking a lot lately about your advice."

"Um—what advice?"

"You know what you always say about taking risks and going after what you want?"

She did say that fairly often. "Well, yes…"

"What's your advice for when a guy wants something very badly, but the risks are damned high?"

"I guess that would depend on how much you're willing to lose," she answered very softly.

He searched her face, and his expression wasn't hard to read that time as he weighed his options. And then he sighed lightly, dropped his hand, and moved an inch backward. "Some things are just too valuable to gamble on."

She reached out and caught his shirt, gathering the fabric just above his heart in her right hand. Giving a little tug, she brought him back to within touching proximity. "Some risks are worth taking."

She lifted her face as he lowered his. He hesitated a breath away from her mouth, as if realizing—as she was—that everything between them would change once their lips touched. As worrisome as that thought was, she made no attempt to draw away when he closed that short distance.

There was no first-kiss tentativeness, no fumbling or awkwardness. Ron's mouth closed over hers with the confidence of intimate acquaintance. And her entire being responded as if welcoming him home. Her fingers tightened spasmodically on his shirt, holding him in place. Her eyes closed, allowing her to concentrate solely on the feel of him, the taste of him, the warmth of him. All sensations she would have sworn she'd experienced many times before.

How could it feel this right when a wary little voice inside her kept screaming warnings?

He lifted his head. Eventually. Slowly. And though she was tempted to tangle her hands in his hair and keep him there, she allowed him to back away.

"Thanks for dinner," he said, inching toward the exit.

He was running. Maybe he needed to process what had just happened between them. She knew she did. "You're welcome."

Had she known when she'd invited him that there was a chance something like this could happen?

She suspected she had.

She followed him to the door. "I'll see you at lecture tomorrow."

He nodded. "Yeah. See ya."

His expression shuttered now, he opened the door and stepped out.

Holding the open door, she spoke impulsively. "Ron?"

He looked over his shoulder. "Yeah?"

"Nothing has to change between us, you know."

He gave her a faint, crooked smile, so different from his usual cocky grins. "We both know it has already changed, Haley."

Biting her lip in a silent acknowledgment of his point, she closed the door between them.

Okay, so she and Ron had kissed. And she couldn't deny that she was the one who'd initiated it when he'd been on the verge of backing off.

Lying in her bed, staring sleeplessly at the darkened ceiling, she replayed the entire scene, and certainly not for the first time since he'd left a few hours earlier.

She supposed it had been inevitable. That kiss had been building for a while. Since Georgia McMillan had put the idea in their heads? Or had she merely commented on something that had been simmering between them almost from the beginning?

She already knew the answer to that rhetorical question.

So, she was drawn to Ron. And vice versa. More than a casual attraction—the heat between them had built from the start. Sometimes erupting in temper, other times in barely suppressed temptation.

Restlessly rearranging her pillows, she pulled the sheet to her chin. Like Ron, she worried about doing anything that would permanently affect their friendship. Attraction or no, she valued the connection between them. The shared memories, the mutual support and encouragement. The bond that had been forged among the five study friends during those sometimes nightmarish first two years. The celebrations of accomplishments and milestones. Each of her friends was precious to her.

She had a pretty good track record of staying on good terms with former lovers, she reminded herself. She and Kris had parted on very amicable terms, and she still remained in loose contact with her two college boyfriends. So even if she and Ron allowed themselves to explore the feelings between them, it didn't mean they couldn't remain friends when it ended.

And it would end, she thought, punching her pillow. There were so many strikes against them. Their differing personalities. The career commitments they had made that would keep them busy for several years yet before they could even begin their practices. Not to mention Ron's notorious reluctance to make a full commitment to anything. Or anyone, for that matter. She remembered hearing him make several only half-joking comments about being a confirmed bachelor who valued his independence.

It wasn't as if she was looking for anything serious, herself. She had another year and a half of medical school, including preparation for the Step 2 exams. Then five years of residency, followed by getting established in her chosen career. She certainly wasn't saying she wouldn't make a commitment to anyone during the next seven years, but she didn't think it would be soon. Nor was it likely to be with a man whose stated philosophy was, "If it's not working out, just walk away."

So…a temporary affair, perhaps. With the understanding from the start that it was nothing more. Wasn't that what she'd had with Kris? They'd had fun for a while, then gone their own ways, both emotionally richer for the experiences they had shared. They hadn't given up and walked away—not the way Ron defined walking away, anyway.

Or maybe it wouldn't even go that far. Maybe a few kisses would satisfy the itch, or the curiosity, or whatever it was drawing them together. They could play it by ear. See what happened. She could do that without risking too much, as long as she kept the limitations in mind from the start.

It wasn't as if she was falling in love or anything.

Flipping again, she gave the pillow another hard punch.

He wasn't going to rush this. Fighting his characteristic impulsiveness and impatience, Ron was determined to take things slow with Haley. They'd had two years to get to know each other as friends; now they had plenty of time to explore any new options between them.

He greeted her in the students' room the morning after The Kiss with his usual teasing remarks, neither pretending the incident hadn't happened nor making any specific reference to it. Though her cheeks were a bit pinker than usual, she responded in the same way, chatting easily with him, laughing or groaning at his jokes, even punching his arm once, making him chuckle.

He glanced at his watch. "Time to get back to work."

"Yeah, me, too. See you later, Ron."

"Want to have dinner together after work? Maybe study a little?"

Her hesitation might not have even been noticeable to anyone else. Her smile might have looked entirely natural to someone who didn't know her as well as he did. Which made it all the more satisfying when she nodded and said, "Sure. I'll meet you after work."

One step at a time, he told himself, tucking his stethoscope more snugly into his pocket and heading for the wards. They'd shared the first kiss, and now they needed to spend more time together—not as classmates or study partners, but as a potential couple.

Taking it slow—but definitely taking it forward. Satisfied with that observation, he turned his attention to his young patients.

* * *

Mia's birthday was the last Saturday in September, and Connor invited everyone to their house for a birthday barbecue. He told Ron it was the first time since he'd started medical school that he had time to properly celebrate Mia's birthday. This time he wanted to do it right.

He invited the study group, of course. He'd also extended invitations to a few of his and Mia's coworkers from the school where they'd both taught before he'd started medical school and she'd entered graduate school to obtain her doctorate in education. A few other mutual friends of Connor and Mia's rounded out the sixteen-person guest list.

Haley, of course, had volunteered to help with the party. It wasn't a surprise affair, but Haley wanted to make sure Mia didn't have to go to any extra effort for her own birthday. Though Connor said he had everything under control, he'd asked Haley to meet with him briefly the Wednesday afternoon prior to the event to go over his list and make sure he hadn't forgotten anything, just as a precaution. He'd told her to bring Ron along so the three of them could chat a little before the party, where he would be too busy hosting to have much time for catching up.

Connor was waiting at the coffee shop when they arrived. Seated at a small table with three chairs, he sipped from a steaming cup as he made notes on a pad in front of him. He looked up with a smile when they walked in. Standing, he brushed a light kiss over Haley's cheek and shook Ron's hand.

Ron watched Haley and Connor while he placed an order for Haley's latte and his espresso. Connor had obviously spoken literally when he'd referred to his list. Haley had her head bent over the pad of notes and was involved in a spirited discussion with their friend. Ron figured there would be no details overlooked by the time Haley and Connor were finished today.

They were talking about food for the party when he carried the two steaming drinks to the table, setting Haley's latte in front of her. She looked up with a slightly distracted smile. "Thanks, Ron."

Immediately turning her attention back to Connor, she said, "I'll bring enough of the broccoli slaw for twenty people. That should be plenty."

"You're sure it's not too much trouble?"

"I wouldn't have volunteered if it were too much trouble."

Connor smiled at her. "I really do appreciate it. Mia loves your slaw."

"You're sure there's nothing I can bring?" Ron asked. "I really wouldn't mind picking up some drinks or something."

"All taken care of," Connor assured him gratefully. "But thanks."

"I'm still amazed that everyone's free that afternoon," Haley commented after taking a cautious sip of her beverage. "It's pretty much a miracle these days."

"No kidding. With the five of us on different rotations, it's hard to be sure when anyone has the same Saturday off. Not to mention my own crazy schedule right now, with me in ob-gyn and Mia buried up to her neck in classes and assignments, and Alexis enrolled in after-school dance classes and soccer—let's just say things are sort of hectic at the Hayes house these days."

"And what's new about that?" Ron teased.

Connor's home life had been complicated for as long as Ron had known him. Before his first semester of med school was half over, Connor had learned he was fully responsible for a six-year-old daughter whose existence had been a secret to him until that time. Then he'd realized he was falling in love with Mia, who'd moved in to help him with Alexis.

Connor had known Mia for several years as a friend and coworker before he'd realized his feelings for her were more than platonic.

That thought made Ron glance at Haley, who was already going over the list one more time with Connor.

Finally reassured everything was on track, Connor folded the list and stuck it into his computer bag. "You know you're both welcome to bring guests, if you like. There will be plenty of food for everyone."

Ron shook his head. "Haley and I will come together."

Haley shot him a look and he almost winced. She didn't have to say a word to let him know she wasn't pleased he'd made that decision without consulting her first.

As if sensing an undercurrent between them, Connor looked quickly from Haley to Ron. His only response was a nod, and then a change of subject when he asked how their weeks were going in the general peds wards.

Hoping he hadn't just set their progress back a step, Ron made an extra effort to be amusing during the remainder of his and Haley's short visit with Connor. He was rewarded with smiles and a couple of laughs from her. He was even ridiculously pleased when one of his outrageous comments elicited a punch on his arm, proving he really was pathetic when it came to Haley.

Taking it slow, he reminded himself. But still taking it forward. That was all he could ask, for now.

Chapter Six

No one seemed to find it odd that Haley and Ron arrived at the birthday party together. Nor that they'd gone in together on a birthday gift for Mia. That had been Ron's idea. Saying he had no clue what to get on his own, he'd convinced Haley they could get something nicer if they pooled their money—and if she made the selection. She'd purchased a very pretty scarf and signed her name and Ron's on a casually humorously birthday card. Everyone knew she and Ron were on the same rotation and were spending time together on the wards, so she figured no one would read too much into them carpooling and gift-pooling.

Though she and Ron were now spending quite a bit of time together out of the hospital, too, she wasn't quite ready to announce that they were seeing each other as more than study buddies.

They weren't rushing into anything. The full extent of their relationship at this point was having dinner together and studying together after work. There had been a few more kisses. Carefully controlled, but each a little more heated than the last. She thought Ron was trying to be careful not to move too fast, not to derail this...whatever it was...before it started. She didn't think he was deliberately trying to whet her appetite, or to leave her frustrated and impatient for more. But if that *had* been his intention, he'd have achieved exactly what he'd hoped.

She could hardly look at Ron now without remembering how it felt to be close to him. How warm and solid he felt pressed against her. She found herself daydreaming at odd times about the spicy scent of his aftershave. The springy feel of his thick hair wrapped around her fingers. The way his lips were both firm and soft when they moved against hers. And she spent entirely too much of her free time wondering when—or if—they would progress beyond kisses. Imagining what it would be like when they did.

Maybe that was what he hoped to accomplish, after all.

They were noticeably hesitant to talk about what might be developing between them. They laughed a lot when they were together. Talked about work. Chatted about their mutual friends. Studied. She talked some about her family and her background; he seemed to enjoy hearing stories about her past, but he was still very reticent about his own. She figured that would come in time.

They didn't talk about the future beyond the next rotation.

She figured Ron was no more ready than she was to go public as a potential couple...or whatever they were, even though he'd been awfully quick to announce they would be arriving together when Connor had suggested they could bring other guests. She was prepared to act that afternoon as if nothing at all had changed between them, and she assumed he would, too.

She was right...to a point.

It was a beautiful afternoon. A crisp hint of autumn in the clear air. The sky a rich blue dotted with fluffy white clouds. Brightly colored balloons hovering above the long, folding-leg table Connor had set up to hold the plates of food. A few people sat around the family's picnic table to eat, but almost everyone sat in folding chairs, holding their well-filled plates in their laps. James hadn't been able to make it, being on call at the hospital that afternoon, but the rest of the gang was there.

After everyone had eaten, Connor brought out a beautifully decorated cake he'd ordered from a bakery Haley had recommended. Everyone sang Happy Birthday to Mia, who accepted Alexis's eagerly offered assistance with blowing out the candles. All the guests agreed that the cake tasted as good as it looked.

While Ron helped Connor and some of the other guys clear away the barbecue equipment, Haley was gathering trash into a large plastic bag when Drew Maples caught up with her to stuff a couple of crumpled paper napkins into the bag. "I caught these blowing across the grass."

She smiled at him. "Thanks."

She'd met Drew earlier. In his mid-thirties, he was of average height and appearance, but had an infectious laugh that made Haley smile when she heard it, just as it seemed to do everyone else. He was Alexis's soccer coach, and had become quite friendly with Connor and Mia. He was a single dad; his lively eight-year-old son was romping around the outskirts of the birthday party, kicking a soccer ball with Alexis and her best friend, McKenzie, whose mother was busily stretching plastic wrap across bowls of leftovers.

"So you're one of Connor's medical student friends?"

Tossing a paper plate into the bag, she nodded. "Yes, I am."

"What kind of medicine do you want to practice?"

It was a common question when people found out she was in medical school. Most people seemed to think every medical student started training with a specific goal in mind; the ones who did enter with a plan often changed their mind sometime during their classes and rotations.

"I haven't decided for certain yet," she replied, as she usually did. It was too complicated to explain all the options she was currently considering.

"Connor seems pretty set on family practice."

"Yes. He'll be good at it."

"I think so, too."

"So you coach soccer," she said, because he seemed to expect her to continue the conversation.

"Yeah. But that's just a hobby. In my real life, I'm a heating and air-conditioning technician."

Tying the drawstring at the top of the filled garbage bag, she glanced at the little boy now climbing on Alexis's playground set. "Your son is very cute. He certainly plays well with Alexis and McKenzie."

He followed her to the large garbage can on one corner of the patio, lifting the lid for her so she could deposit the bag. "Yeah, he's a good kid. He stays with me on weekends, and with his mom during the weeks. Doesn't give either of us any trouble. Hope that doesn't change as he gets older."

She smiled. "I'm sure he'll be fine."

"Are you from around here?"

"I grew up in Russellville."

"Yeah? I'm from Morrilton, myself. We were practically neighbors."

He was definitely flirting. Keeping her smile friendly but just a little distant, she motioned toward the big tub filled with melting ice and a few remaining cans of soda. "I think I'll have a diet cola. Would you like something?"

"No, but let me get one for you. Diet, you say?"

Haley thought Ron was still occupied with the other guys, so she was a bit surprised when he appeared suddenly at her side, a diet soda in his hand. "Thought you might be thirsty," he said, offering it to her.

"Thank you."

Nodding cordially to Drew, Ron spoke to Haley again. "Alexis just told me that Connor and Mia are taking her and McKenzie to the state fair next weekend. She's really excited about it."

Remembering family outings to the state fair from her own childhood, Haley smiled. "I'm sure she is."

"You and I should go while it's in town. That's something we haven't done together yet."

It wasn't so much the words as the tone that took her back. He smiled as he spoke, showing a lot of teeth—apparently aimed directly at Drew, whose own smile had faded.

Drew took a step backward. "Excuse me, I think my son is signaling for me."

Haley spun on one heel. "Ron—"

"Haley, Ron, come on." Alexis skidded to a stop beside them, nearly crashing right into Ron, who caught her with a laugh. "She's going to open her presents now."

"I'll talk to you later," Haley said beneath her voice to Ron as they moved toward the table where Mia had been seated behind a stack of gifts.

He grimaced, but stayed close by her side when they rejoined the others.

"Okay, let's have it."

Ron stood in the center of her living room, visibly braced for whatever was to come. Haley didn't bother with prevarications, nor did she have to ask him to clarify what he meant by the demand. She had deliberately kept the conversation neutral on the way from the birthday party, not wanting to get into a serious discussion in the car. She'd known Ron was aware she was only procrastinating.

"What was that performance you put on in front of Drew this afternoon?" she asked, planting her hands on her hips as she faced him.

He shoved a hand through his breeze-tossed sandy hair. "It wasn't a performance. He was making an obvious play for you, and I blocked it. That's all."

She huffed. "I am not a football."

His lips quirked, but she was sure he knew better than to laugh. "No."

"And I am perfectly capable of deflecting passes, myself," she went on, unintentionally continuing the metaphor. "I didn't need you stepping in to make both me and Drew feel awkward."

The hints of amusement left Ron's face then. "He should have felt awkward. It was damned rude of him to corner you like that at a party for a friend. Especially considering you'd come with a date."

"I guess he knew I'd ridden to the party with you, but I doubt he or anyone else was aware that we were there...well, together. Not until you decided to act like you were marking your territory, anyway."

His brows drew together. "Maybe we should have made it clearer from the start—to everyone—that we weren't just carpooling."

"Like a general announcement, you mean?" she asked with more than a touch of sarcasm.

He responded more seriously than she'd expected. "Yeah. Something like that."

She took a tiny step backward, a physical enactment of her emotional response. "We're nowhere close to being ready for that step."

His frown deepened. "What? Letting people know we're seeing each other? That we enjoy doing more together than just studying? That we're attracted to each other?"

"I just think it's best if we don't mention to the others that anything is different from the way it's always been between us. It's all still too new. Too...well, experimental."

"Experimental." He repeated her ill-chosen word with a tone of distaste.

Flushing a little, she shook her head. "That's not exactly the word I meant. What I'm trying to say is that I don't want to make things uncomfortable with our friends when we get together in the future."

"If things don't work out between us, you mean."

"For *any* reason."

Tired of being on the defensive when he was the one who'd gotten out of line that day, she lifted her chin. "We haven't even talked, ourselves, about what's changing between us. All we've done so far is share a few dinners and a few kisses. That's hardly enough to change everything."

Nor for him to start acting like she was now off the market when it came to other men, she added silently. True, she'd had no interest in responding to Drew's flirting, but still...

"You're right," Ron surprised her by saying a bit too evenly.

"I am?"

He nodded, taking a step toward her to close the distance she'd put deliberately between them. "A few kisses isn't enough to change everything."

"Well, yes, that's what I just said. I..."

His hands closed around her forearms and he pulled her toward him with a little more intensity than usual. There was no hint of the clown in his eyes when he lowered his head.

"A change is on the way," he warned, just before his lips closed over hers.

This kiss was definitely different. Sensations exploded inside her when he deepened the embrace, taking her mouth with a thorough, masculine confidence that made every feminine cell inside her spring to life. His tongue thrust between her lips, exploring and claiming. His arms were strong around her, holding her so tightly against him she couldn't possibly be unaware of his hunger for her.

She locked her arms around his neck and strained to get closer, her tongue parrying his with an equal fervor. All the impatient curiosity building inside her for the past few weeks fueled her response to this embrace, urging her to push on, to explore, to finally have her answer to the question that had been haunting her. What would it be like when they finally came together?

This preview was telling her it was going to be amazing. Perhaps life changing. And that thought scared her as much as it thrilled her.

Ron's hands slid down her hips, moving inward to cup her bottom, to fit her even more snugly against him. He tilted his head to taste her lips from a new angle. She locked her fingers in his hair, holding him there while she thoroughly explored every inch of his mouth.

Her tingling breasts flattened against his broad chest, she rocked lightly against him, eliciting a groan from him. His fingers dug spasmodically into her, and this time the moan was hers.

He tore his mouth from hers with a gasp. "Haley—"

Drawing a deep, hitching breath, she pushed lightly against him. He released her immediately, a kaleidoscope of emotions shifting through his darkened blue eyes.

Everything was changing. Had already changed.

Without a word, she held out a hand to him, pleased that it was relatively steady.

Ron glanced from that offered hand to her face. He must have read the invitation in her expression. He took her hand in a grip that was just short of painful before deliberately loosening his grasp.

Haley turned and led him to her bedroom.

More kisses. More leisurely, yet increasingly urgent, caresses. Exploring touches. Encouraging murmurs.

Clothing fell to the floor, tangled in piles of his and hers. A sweep of Ron's hand and the decorative throw pillows from her bed tumbled on top of the clothing.

What might have been a long time later—or maybe only minutes—Ron hovered over her, his hair tousled around his face, which was taut with need and restraint. The dimmed bedside lamp threw shadows across his features, changing his appearance in some way. Or was she simply seeing him differently now?

She reached up to stroke a lock of hair out of his eyes. Though her entire body quivered with eager need, she didn't try to rush him. She savored the moment. The anticipation. The certainty that the wait would be justified.

He pressed his lips lightly against her cheek, trailing a line of kisses to her mouth, which he took tenderly this time, weakening whatever defenses she might have had left against him. Her hand slid to the back of his head, her fingers burying themselves in his hair.

His bare skin was so warm against hers, as if heated by a low-grade fever. She knew the heat had nothing to do with illness. She suspected her own skin felt as warm to his prowling hands.

Poised to join them, he hesitated one last time, looking down at her as if to be sure she hadn't changed her mind. For just a fleeting moment, she asked herself what on earth she was doing. This was Ron! Her friend, her study partner, her sometimes squabble mate. The man who exasperated her with his lack of willingness to fully commit, who teased her mercilessly until she snapped at him, who she'd always thought of as a charming, walking heartache.

Ron.

The man whose touch made her yearn for more.

Smiling mistily, she arched to welcome him. With a muffled groan, he accepted the invitation.

Ron's mood was so good for the next few days that nearly everyone he encountered seemed compelled to comment on his cheery attitude. He flirted more vigorously with the female staff, joked with the guys, teased with his patients, reassured and comforted their families.

Maybe he felt so confident because things were going so well at work—he'd even received a few grudging compliments from his resident and attending. He was actually starting to feel like a physician—or at least, a potential one. And while he knew things could take a fast downturn in that respect, with one embarrassing gaffe or one poorly timed moment of forgetfulness, he decided to enjoy his good fortune while it lasted.

He behaved himself as best he could around Haley, at least when other people were around. She was extremely busy during those days and they barely had time to greet each other in the hallways, but he relished the new warm gleam in her eyes when she saw him. At least, he thought he saw a new warmth there. He hoped he wasn't simply projecting his own feelings onto her.

For the first time in more years than he could remember, Ron was almost giddily optimistic about his future. He was going to be a doctor, he would help people—kids...and he had good reason to believe that Haley would be very much a part of that fulfilling future. There was nothing more he could ask for now.

Watching Haley laughing with one of the nurses over a particularly amusing patient, he swallowed hard on a sudden wave of unease. It had been so long since he'd allowed himself to want anything this badly. Since he'd invested so much of himself in anything, knowing that it wouldn't be so easy to walk away this time.

He'd forgotten how much fear could be embedded in hope.

Shaken out of his reverie by a summons from his resident, he told himself to push the worries aside and focus on the present. After all, it was Haley who always encouraged him to expect the best, to prepare only for success and not to anticipate failure.

He was looking forward to practicing what she preached.

Haley hadn't been involved in the initial planning, so she wasn't sure quite how it had come about, but the weekend after Mia's party, she found herself on a double date to the state fair with Ron, James and James's friend, Elissa Copeland. It turned out that James had never actually been to the fair, and Ron seemed to think it was his mission to remedy that grievous situation. Ron had convinced Haley to join him in that endeavor—which hadn't been too difficult, she admitted to herself as they climbed out of his car in the fairgrounds parking lot.

Elissa seemed nice enough, if a little too reserved. She was tall, slender, attractive, her hair expensively colored to a multitoned warm blond, her face perfectly made up. She'd dressed appropriately for the occasion—slim jeans and a thin, form-fitting orange sweater with an orange-and-brown cardigan tied around her shoulders in preparation for the after-sundown temperature drop. She and James made a striking couple, with him being so dark and broodingly handsome.

Ron wore faded jeans with a gray medical school sweatshirt. Haley, too, had donned jeans, along with a red hoodie with red-and-white striped sleeves. She'd thought she looked sort of cute and sporty when she'd left the house; seeing Elissa made her feel just a little grubby. She pushed that feeling aside with rueful self-reproach, reminding herself that this wasn't a fashion competition. Especially since a predominant pattern seen at the fair was camo, and many of the people in attendance were teenagers dressed in all sorts of odd and attention-begging garb.

Ron took her hand as they joined the crowd streaming in through the gates of the fairgrounds. He was keeping them from becoming separated, true, but he also seemed to enjoy the contact. He wasn't even pretending tonight that they were still merely friends.

She wasn't sure if he'd said anything to James about the change in their relationship. She and Ron had been lovers only for a week. It was still too new for her to be casual about it, or comfortable sharing the news with everyone else. She hadn't yet mentioned the change to her mom or even her own best friend, Anne. She'd been trying to decide exactly how to announce that her relationship with Ron had gone to a new level, but no one should expect wedding bells anytime in the future.

It was very much the same sort of relationship she'd had with Kris. Light. Fun. Nothing serious. It was just a little trickier this time. Kris hadn't been part of her close circle of friends, so his absence was hardly noticeable in her life.

She supposed her study group was already drifting onto different paths as they moved through the latter half of medical school, and they would go their own ways after graduation, but she hated to think she couldn't remain friends with all of them, wherever their careers took them. She couldn't bear to think of a future without Ron in it, though she wanted to believe that was only a sign of how much she valued his friendship.

Trying to hear each other speak over the cacophony of loud music, amplified game barkers, screaming rides and shrieking children, the two couples wandered down the fairway, taking in the sights. The sun was just setting, and the colorful lights on the fairgrounds glared against the purple sky. The musky scent of the surrounding animal barns blended with the aromas of popped corn and grilled turkey legs and fried dough and beer, taking Haley straight back to her childhood. Her mouth was already beginning to water for a fatty, blatantly unhealthy meal.

"So what do y'all want?" Ron asked, pausing in the center of a grouping of concession trailers and motioning toward some of the more garish signs. "Chocolate covered bacon? Gator on a stick? Fried candy bars?"

Elissa studied the offerings with an almost visible shudder. "Seriously? People eat that stuff?"

Because they were surrounded by people eating "that stuff," none of the others bothered to respond.

They found a food vendor operating from beneath a pavilion covering quite a few wood-slatted picnic tables, and they decided to eat there. Haley and Ron ordered Cajun chicken wings and grilled corn cobs slathered with melted butter and dusted with spicy seasoning. James and Elissa settled on cheeseburgers, though Elissa barely touched hers.

It felt good to sit for a few minutes, Haley thought with a little sigh. She'd been at the hospital at seven that morning and had barely stopped running since, getting home just in time to change for this outing.

During the meal, Haley discovered that Elissa was a pharmacy student at the medical school. Elissa and James had met in the cafeteria, and had dated a couple of times. They seemed to get along well, but Haley saw no real chemistry between them. James was as polite and considerate with Elissa as he was with everyone else. She treated him pretty much the same way, though Haley suspected that Elissa was a bit more invested in him. But Haley would freely admit that she couldn't even guess what James was looking for in a mate.

"How long have the two of you been dating?" Elissa asked Haley, nodding toward Ron as she spoke. James looked as though he wouldn't mind hearing the answer to that question, himself.

"Not long," Haley said, glancing at Ron before looking back at the other woman. "But we've been friends for quite a while. How's your burger?"

"Greasy."

James wiped his mouth on a paper napkin. "Mine's pretty good."

Ron grinned. "Grease is the best part of fair food, right, James?"

James didn't look quite convinced, but he nodded obligingly.

Elissa wasn't ready to have her conversational topic derailed. "It's sort of tricky dating a classmate, isn't it?"

Wiping her fingers, Haley began to gather her trash to carry to the nearest receptacle. "No, not really. We're equals. It isn't like one of us is a resident or attending and the other a student, or any other sticky balance of power issue."

"No, I just meant I've heard it's sometimes difficult for couples to get residencies in the same place. Especially if they're particularly exclusive residencies. Which means both having to settle for alternate choices."

Haley's heart gave a hard thump, though she kept her smile bland. "Oh, we're a long way from choosing residencies. We still have to get through the rest of our peds rotation."

And she had no intention of talking about her future—with or without Ron—with Elissa tonight. Standing, she tossed her trash into the receptacle and looked at Ron. "Want to ride the Ferris wheel?"

He rose with a laugh, though his eyes were hard to read when they swept her face. "I'll ride the Ferris wheel if you'll ride the pirate ship with me."

She hated the pirate ship. But she'd rather ride that than continue this particular discussion. "It's a deal."

Elissa sighed lightly, but stood to join the others as they left the dining pavilion.

Though James and Elissa remained on the ground, Haley and Ron rode the Ferris wheel. Ignoring the other riders in the big gondola, Ron kissed her at the top, assuring her it was tradition to do so. Grinning, a teenage boy on the opposite seat took the opportunity to steal a kiss from the blushing girl with him.

The huge, wildly swinging pirate ship made Haley close her eyes and cling for dear life to Ron's arm. Laughing, he pulled her close on the pretext of keeping her safe. She decided maybe she didn't dislike that particular ride so much, after all.

James was nearly toppled by a runaway preschooler when they moved on down the fairway. He caught the little redhead just before the collision, keeping a hand on the laughing tot while the four of them looked around for the adult in charge of him. Only moments behind the boy, a fresh-faced young redhead in her early twenties ran toward them.

"I'm sorry," she said breathlessly. "I let my nephew out of his stroller just for a moment so I could clean out some popcorn he spilled, and he took off running."

"No problem." James handed over the boy with one of his lazily gorgeous smiles, making the redhead blink rather dazedly. Haley didn't blame her. When James turned on the charm, every woman in the vicinity responded with an instinctive sigh. She wasn't totally immune to it, herself, though she had never been drawn to James in a romantic way.

Ron was the one whose grins made her heart skip beats, she mused, looking at Ron from beneath her eyelashes. He was ruffling the little boy's hair, making the child shriek with laughter. He was so good with children. He'd be a wonderful pediatrician.

Remembering the things Elissa had said, she wondered where he was considering applying for his residency program. And whether there was a triple-board program wherever he might end up.

She forced that errant thought aside as the redhead held out her hand to the boy. "Come on, Jack. You're going back in your stroller. Your mom's probably wondering where you are. Thanks for catching him," she added to James, glancing at him over her shoulder when she led the child away.

James nodded. His gaze seemed to linger for a moment on the redhead's slender back before he courteously returned his attention to his companions.

After they had wandered through the Arts and Crafts Building and the Hall of Industry, Ron decided he wanted to go on one more ride. When Haley declined, he dared James to join him in a basket that would be lifted high in the air, then flipped over a few times. James didn't look overly enthusiastic, but he accepted the dare. He and Ron got in line, leaving Haley to try to make conversation with Elissa.

"Are you having a good time?" she asked after swallowing a bite of the caramel-covered apple in her hand.

Sidestepping a rambunctious toddler carrying a sticky, cotton-candy cone, Elissa gave a little shrug that might have held a slight apology. "The fair's not really my thing," she said candidly. "I'd have preferred a nice restaurant or a club. But it hasn't been too bad. What about you?"

Faint praise, indeed. Haley smiled. "I enjoy anything that gets me out of my apartment and away from studying for a few hours. It seems like that's all I've done for the past two and a half years. I'm sure you know the feeling. You must have to study a lot, too."

Elissa nodded. "Yes. It's more difficult than I expected, actually. I'll be glad to finish."

"How much longer?"

"Another year."

"Same here."

"Yes, I know." Elissa motioned vaguely toward James.

"Oh. Of course."

Elissa edged a bit closer. "Can you tell me a little more about him? James, I mean. This is our third date and I still know next to nothing about him, except that his parents are academics and he already has a Ph.D. in microbiology."

"What do you want to know?"

"Oh, you know." She glanced over to make sure James and Ron were still in line for the ride, safely out of hearing. "Has he dated a lot during medical school? Is he looking for permanence or just playing the field? It's hard for me to tell."

"Sorry, I can't answer any of that," Haley replied honestly. "James has been a good friend and study partner, but he keeps his private life to himself, for the most part. I know he's brought a few dates to school social events, but I can't tell you much more than that."

"Dates," Elissa repeated. "So there hasn't been anyone serious since you've known him?"

"Not as far as I'm aware."

She had no intention of saying more than that. Anything else of a personal nature Elissa wanted to know about James, she would have to ask him herself. Haley took another bite of her juicy apple, trying not to get the caramel coating all over her face.

Maybe Elissa got the unspoken message. She nodded and let the subject drop, moving slightly away again.

A group of noisy teenagers ran up to the ride entrance, jostling Haley's elbow. She tried to move out of their way, though the area was already almost shoulder to shoulder with people stopping to watch the shrieking riders or trying to pass toward the children's ride section or surrounding games and concessions.

"Let's go on this one," one of the three boys in the group of seven insisted, pointing toward the ride Ron and James were just climbing into.

The four girls squealed and giggled and dithered, but all were persuaded to get in line. One boy hung back, coughing into his hand. "Y'all go ahead. I just ate that giant funnel cake with chocolate topping. I don't want to lose it when the ride starts flipping over."

His friends teased him, using mildly profane language, but he merely waved them on, trying to suppress another cough. Because of the limited space, he stood rather close to Haley as he watched his friends. Even over the noises surrounding them, she could hear the wheezy edge to his increasingly labored breathing.

She bit her lip to keep her concern to herself. Medical students were too prone to offer unsolicited advice, she reminded herself. She should just mind her own business.

Looking out of the corner of her eye, she decided he might have been fifteen. Skinny, his face a little pale beneath the scattered zits, his hair fashionably shaggy and limp. He gave another wheezy cough. Because she'd spent two weeks on the pediatric pulmonology ward, she knew the sound of asthma when she heard it. The dust and animal dander and cigarette smoke and other pollutants at the fairgrounds had to be hard on asthma and other breathing disorders.

Because his wheezing seemed to be getting worse and she simply couldn't stand it any longer, she finally turned to him. "Do you have an inhaler?"

He blinked and looked around as though checking to make sure she was talking to him. "Uh—yeah," he mumbled, smothering another cough.

"Don't you think you should use it? All the stuff in the air here can't be good for your breathing."

He glanced quickly at his friends. "I don't want to use an inhaler right here in front of everyone. They'd think I was a nerd."

Kids, she thought with a suppressed sigh. Specifically, male kids. Did he really think it would be cooler to succumb to a full-out asthma attack than to ward it off with his inhaler?

"See that little alleyway between the two games?" she asked, nodding toward her right.

Following her glance, he nodded.

"Duck in there and use your inhaler. My friend and I will stand in front of the opening so no one can see you. Won't we, Elissa?"

Elissa seemed a little startled, but nodded with a shrug. "Sure. Why not?"

After only a momentary hesitation, the boy agreed.

Standing with their backs turned to the narrow opening, Haley and Elissa waited until they'd heard the boy take a couple of deep hits on his inhaler before moving away. He coughed a couple of times when he rejoined them, but already Haley could hear the wheezing subsiding a little.

"Thanks," he mumbled, shuffling a sneakered foot against the littered asphalt.

"You're welcome. I assume you know the warning signs if your asthma is really starting to get out of control?"

He nodded. "I'll be careful."

She doubted that, but she'd done all she could—probably more than she should have. "Have a good time."

He grinned. "I'm going to tell the guys I've been hitting on you two hotties."

She laughed. "If I were ten years younger, I'd take you up on that."

Grinning, he swaggered toward his pals, who were watching him in open curiosity now. Haley noted that the other boys looked rather impressed—exactly what her asthmatic friend had hoped to accomplish, she thought with a chuckle.

A little disheveled from the wild ride, Ron and James rejoined them then. Ron glanced from Haley to the departing teen. "What have you been up to?"

"Flirting," she answered with a smiling look toward Elissa. "We're certified hotties, you know."

Elissa actually returned a full smile, which made her look so pretty that Haley could see why James had asked her out.

Ron slung an arm around Haley's shoulders. "You don't have to tell me you're hot. I've been aware of it for quite some time."

Flushing a little in pleasure, she let her speculation about James and Elissa fade to the back of her mind.

Ron would have been perfectly happy to leave the fairgrounds without playing any of the carnival games lining the fairway. He'd nodded cordially to the barkers and game operators as he'd passed, but he had no desire to try to conquer their house-slanted challenges.

He'd only wanted an excuse to spend an evening out with Haley, he admitted to himself, smiling down at her as they ambled toward the exit. True, he'd suggested the fair on impulse at Mia's party partially as a way to make it clear to the encroaching Drew that Haley wasn't available. But then James had commented that he'd never actually been to the fair, and Ron had seized on the idea of making it a double date. His way of announcing to everyone—Haley, included—that he saw them as a couple now, he supposed.

He'd had a great time on this outing with her. He loved it when she laughed, and she'd laughed a lot tonight. She needed to play occasionally rather than focus all the time on excelling in her education. He figured he was the best choice to make sure she took time for frivolities.

Surprisingly enough, it was Elissa who talked them into trying a few of the games on their way out of the fairgrounds. "Win me a stuffed animal?" she asked James, waving toward some colorful toys dangling from beneath a brightly lit awning.

He glanced at the game—a challenge to toss a small basketball through a barely larger hoop only a few feet away—and shrugged. "Sure. Looks easy enough."

Ron groaned. "Looks are definitely deceiving when it comes to carnival games, buddy. The games always favor the house."

James lifted an eyebrow. "They're fixed?"

"Not necessarily. Just designed to look much easier than they are. The way that hoop is shaped, you have to hit it at exactly the right spot to get the ball through."

A buxom, bleached-blonde in a very tight T-shirt passed by them, carrying a giant purple bear. A cowboy in tight jeans and denim shirt strutted beside her, toting a big yellow bear.

"Looks like that guy knows how to win," James commented.

"The guy probably works for the carnival."

James looked intrigued.

"Hey, fellas! Three tries for five bucks!" Seeing that they had paused in front of his booth, the carnie motioned them closer. He tossed a basketball in one hand as he urged them to give it a try.

"Get just one ball through the hoop and win one of the prizes on the wall," he told them, waving a hand toward a display of normal-sized stuffed toys.

James glanced at Elissa, who smiled at him. Probably figured he'd like her to play up to his ego, Ron thought cynically. Elissa was obviously angling for James, but he couldn't tell that his friend was particularly smitten with her in return.

But James was as susceptible to a male ego challenge as the next guy. He reached for his wallet.

Ron sighed.

Ten dollars and six shots later, Elissa's hands were still empty. James gave her a rueful smile, holding up his hands in defeat.

"Told ya," Ron muttered.

The carnie looked at Ron with a slight frown that he immediately smoothed into a toothy grin. "How about you, pal? Think you can show your buddy there how it's done?"

"No, that's okay."

Haley patted his arm. "Don't waste your money, Ron."

"She doesn't think you can do it," the carnie taunted. "Are you gonna take that?"

Ron sighed again. Hell, he had an ego, too. He slapped a five into the carnie's outstretched hand. "Give me the ball."

Three shots. Three hoops. "Pick your prize," he told Elissa. "I'll win Haley one at the next booth."

James was laughing, totally at ease with being shown up by Ron. The bored carnie next to the hoops game perked up.

"Think it's that easy?" he asked Ron. "Can you knock all the bottles completely off the stand with a baseball? All you have to do is clear the stand one time and win a big prize for your lady."

Sounded easy enough. Just knock down the stacked bottles with a baseball. Of course, the rules stated that the bottles had to be completely off the stand, not scattered across it. And that took a direct hit in exactly the right spot to accomplish.

A spot Ron just happened to know.

The bottles flew off the stand with a satisfying clatter. He pointed to a green bear, which he then presented to Haley with a little bow. "Everyone ready to go now?"

All three of his companions studied him with open curiosity. Haley, of course, was the one to ask, "How do you know how to win these games so easily? How much time have you spent at carnivals, anyway?"

"I was a carnie for almost a year," he said with a shrug and a wry smile for the game operator, who gave him a little salute in acknowledgment. "After I dropped out of college the first time."

"You never told me that," Haley said almost accusingly over the head of the green bear.

He added a little swagger to his steps toward the exit. "Sugar, there's a lot I haven't told you."

She punched his biceps.

Laughing, he slung an arm around her shoulders.

He didn't want to think about the past right now. Too many painful memories there. Too many dumb mistakes he didn't want to dwell on now.

The future was still so vague and daunting. He hadn't liked Elissa's questions about residency programs, and her implication that one of them—and no one had to question which one—might have to compromise if they wanted to stay together in the future. He would never allow himself to be responsible for holding Haley back in her chosen career. So he wouldn't think about the future, either.

He would be content, for now, with enjoying every minute he could spend with Haley.

Chapter Seven

Haley and Ron were assigned to the newborn nursery for one week during their pediatrics block. Both found the experience interesting, though they agreed that neonatal medicine was not for them.

As part of the pediatrics team, Haley was called to scrub in on high-risk deliveries. Her initial case was a first-time mother in her mid-thirties whose escalating hypertension had made her doctor decide on a C-section at thirty-four weeks of pregnancy. Careful to remain in the sterile zone, Haley hovered close to the table while the resident, under close observation by the attending physician, wielded the scalpel.

The four-pound, six-ounce boy, still covered in goo, flailed weakly when he was placed into Haley's gloved hands. Staring down at her tiny patient in awe, she carried him carefully, but quickly, to the warmer for cleaning and a stimulating, full-body massage. His Apgar scores would be determined at one and five minutes, possibly again at ten minutes if warranted.

She ran through a quick litany of the factors that contributed to the Apgar score: heart rate, breathing, reflex irritability, activity and appearance. Each factor received a score from zero to two, which were all added up for a total of ten points on the Apgar score, the healthiest of babies. This little guy earned a score of five at one minute, but after suctioning and supplemental oxygen, was up to a seven by five minutes, to everyone's satisfaction. Considering his prematurity and low birth weight, he was reasonably healthy and had a good prognosis.

The boy's mother was also doing well, Haley noted with a quick sideways glance, though the mother was not her concern as a pediatrics student.

Almost three hours after that delivery, Haley and Anne had a few minutes to meet downstairs for a cup of coffee. Haley had lunched with her resident, but Anne, who was on her internal medicine rotation, hadn't yet had a chance to eat. She downed an energy bar while they chatted about the birth Haley had witnessed and some of the cases Anne was monitoring on the adult wards.

Anne glanced at her watch, carefully keeping track of her short break time before she had to report back to her duties. "Long day."

Haley shifted in her chair to stretch out a few kinks. "It has been. Remember back when we used to get eight full hours of uninterrupted sleep? When was the last time? College?"

"High school, more like," Anne answered ruefully. "I was an overachiever in college, too, remember?"

Haley stifled a yawn. "You'd think after almost two and a half years I'd be used to it."

Anne studied her short fingernails. "Ron keeping you out late?"

The question was very casually asked, but more loaded than it seemed on the surface. Haley had finally admitted to her best friend that she was seeing Ron, though as she'd planned, she'd quickly added her caveat about it not being a serious courtship. Anne hadn't looked surprised by the news, but neither had she looked convinced about Haley's definition of a mutually casual affair. At least she hadn't asked any awkward questions; she was too good a friend for that.

Come to think of it, none of the study group members had asked any questions, Haley mused with a slight frown. Connor and James, too, had acted as if they'd been expecting this development. Had her attraction to Ron really been so obvious to them, even before she'd acknowledged it herself?

"We've done a few things. After work. When we aren't studying for shelf exams. Ron thinks it's important to play a little when we can to avoid third-year burnout."

"Sounds like a good plan. Liam and I try to make time for a little fun when we both happen to be in the same town and free for a few hours. My dad thinks a medical student should live, breathe and dream studying, but Liam has convinced me that it's best for both the student and the relationship to try to keep some balance between studying and having a life."

Haley started to remind Anne that she and Ron didn't have a relationship, exactly—certainly not the kind Anne had with her husband—but her pager's beeping interrupted her. She sighed and set down her coffee cup. "Gotta go. I'll see you... well, whenever I see you."

Anne chuckled and waved her off, understanding completely.

The medical school turnout for the Halloween party wasn't quite as good as it had been for the tailgate party in September. Though because grad students, law students, pharmacy and nursing students were also invited, the crowd was large. Haley and Ron attended together, but they were the only ones representing their study group there. Connor and Mia were hosting a Halloween party at their house for Alexis and her friends. Liam was out of the country on an assignment and Anne hadn't been interested in attending without him. And James had simply declined, saying he wasn't interested.

Haley knew James wasn't seeing Elissa anymore, though she didn't know why or whether the parting had been amicable. Maybe he just didn't want to come stag and didn't have anyone he was interested in asking tonight.

She probably wouldn't have come, herself, if she wasn't a class officer. She was really tired, having just completed her outpatient peds rotation. The past two weeks had seen her in a different specialty every day, and her head was still reeling from all the information that had been crammed into it. She just hoped she'd retained enough for her shelf exam.

Because their time had been so limited, she and Ron had rented costumes rather than try to come up with ideas on their own. He chose them as soon as he saw them in the store. To her, they looked like ordinary Western-style clothes. A brown duster coat with faux buckskin pants, suspenders and hip-slung holsters bearing toy revolvers for him, and a long, full-skirted red brocade gown with a snug, low-cut bodice and matching parasol for her. Ron assured her that the costumes were equally appropriate if they were dressed as characters from a cult-favorite, TV "Space Western" that had played for only one season nearly a decade earlier.

"I'm Captain Mal," he said, strutting in his costume, "and you're…well, you're Inara. The, um, paid companion."

She had to chuckle at his description of her character. When she then confessed she'd never seen that particular program, he acted scandalized. He had the whole series on disk, he informed her, as well as the movie that had followed a couple years afterward. He was going to make sure she watched every episode.

She laughed wearily. "As if we have time to watch TV— disks or otherwise. Especially an entire series."

"There are only fourteen episodes and a movie. Maybe we can manage one a week or so."

Which would take them through the next almost four months, she thought with a slight frown. The holidays. Well into the next semester. It was the closest either of them had come to planning for a future together—and that only to watch an old TV series. "Well, we'll see."

He'd looked at her rather oddly, as if hearing something in her tone he couldn't quite interpret, but he'd let the subject drop.

The Halloween party was a little wild, involving more than a few scanty costumes and free-flowing alcohol. Some people found it necessary to relieve the stress of postgraduate training with excessive partying when they had the chance. Haley wasn't one of them. After a couple hours, she was ready to leave.

"Hang on," Ron told her, holding up a finger to indicate one minute. "I just need to ask Hardik something before we go. I'll be right back."

She nodded with a smile. "There's no rush."

He had just stepped away when a tall, slender woman in a fringed flapper dress approached her. "Hi, Haley."

"Hi, Margo. Have I told you how cute you look tonight?"

Margo patted her perfectly waved and styled dark hair. "Thanks. You look nice, too."

Coming from Margo, she supposed that was high praise. "Thank you. Where's your date?"

"He stepped outside to take a phone call. You're here with Ron?"

"Yes. He's over there, talking to Hardik. We're getting ready to leave, actually."

"I won't be here much longer. Watching other people get smashed is hardly my idea of fun."

Margo's idea of fun was being at the head of the class. Making sure all the residents and attendings knew her name. Positioning herself for the most competitive residency and to win as many class awards as possible at graduation.

Deciding exhaustion was making her cranky, Haley felt guilty about those less than gracious thoughts, which made her smile more warmly at her classmate.

Her smile faded a bit when Margo asked, "So, are you and Ron getting serious, or what?"

Haley cocked an eyebrow, the closest she would allow herself to pointing out that it was none of Margo's business.

"The only reason I'm asking is, I'm sort of surprised, you know? I mean, Ron's nice enough—he certainly knows how to make everyone laugh—but…well, he's not exactly serious about getting to the top, is he? Or about anything, for that matter. No offense, but I know you're looking to get into a good residency program and you wouldn't want to throw that away so you can find someplace that will also accept him."

Despite Margo's snotty remark about people getting smashed, she had obviously had more than a few drinks, herself. As blunt as she usually was, this was out of line even for her. Haley replied coldly, "Ron is a very good student and he'll be an excellent doctor, Margo. Believe me, he takes that seriously."

"Someone talking about me?" Ron asked, sliding up beside her with a swish of his long coat.

Wondering how much he might have overheard, Haley searched his face, but couldn't read the expression behind his lazy grin. Margo didn't even have the grace to look abashed that he might have heard her cutting remarks. She merely gave him a cool nod and said she had to go find her escort.

"Ready to go?" Ron asked Haley.

"Definitely," she said, turning on one heel toward the exit.

* * *

Ron shrugged out of the duster coat that had let him pretend for a few hours to be a dashing space cowboy. He tossed it over the back of a chair in Haley's living room and ran a hand through his hair. She'd gone into her bedroom to change out of the long dress, but he could still picture her wearing it.

The red brocade dress, trimmed with silver lace, had dipped low in the front, showing an intriguing amount of creamy cleavage. Fitted snugly to the waist, it had hugged her slender rib cage then draped away from her hips into a long skirt gathered into a bow in the back—right above her very nice tush. Long sleeves and lacy fingerless gloves had made the dress seem more modest than it actually was. She'd curled her brown hair so that it waved around her face beneath a flirty little lace-trimmed hat.

She'd looked both delectable and adorable. He'd told her so more than once that evening, though he wasn't sure she'd taken him seriously.

Ron's not exactly serious about anything. The paraphrase of Margo's snippy contention echoed in his mind, making him scowl. She either hadn't realized he'd heard her or hadn't cared; there hadn't been a hint of apology in her eyes when she'd nodded to him and walked away. Maybe she simply thought she owed no apology for stating what she considered to be indisputable fact.

Or maybe she'd known very well that he could hear her. Had that been her way of subtly warning him not to hold Haley back?

Ron is a very good student and he'll be an excellent doctor.

He supposed Haley had considered herself leaping to his defense, and had said the first words that popped into her head, but it hadn't exactly been a ringing endorsement.

So, what had he wanted her to say? Brooding, he sank onto the couch, pushing at the holster belted around his waist. Had he wanted her to declare her devotion to him? Her undying admiration for him? Had he wanted her to refute Margo's implication that he was too flippant about his studies and his training, that there was nothing he considered worth taking too seriously?

Maybe Haley hadn't said those things because she didn't quite believe them, herself. She had accused him in the past of having the wrong attitude, just because he'd admitted he was prepared to walk away if things didn't work out for him. It wasn't as if his life would be over if he didn't become a physician, he'd argued. He had Plans B, C and D to fall back on—not that he knew what those were, exactly.

Haley had retorted that if he wasn't committed to success at all costs, then he had the wrong attitude about completing this challenging, demanding career path.

Maybe he hadn't been fully committed to medical school at the beginning, he admitted now. Even though he'd worked his butt off to get this far, there had always been a tiny doubt that he'd ever hold that diploma in his hand.

Had he ever fully committed to anything in his life? Had he ever gone into any new endeavor without keeping one eye on the always-present escape hatch?

Would Haley believe him if he told her that he hadn't been looking for an escape from what he'd found with her? He wouldn't hold her back when she was ready to move ahead of him, but he wasn't in any hurry to take an alternate path, either.

She emerged from the bedroom dressed in a pink T-shirt and black yoga pants with a pink stripe down the side. She looked just as adorable as she had in her costume.

"Haley—"

She spoke at the same time, cutting off whatever he might have said in a clumsy attempt to express his feelings. "Do you want any coffee or anything?"

"No, thanks. Had plenty to eat and drink at the party. What I—"

"I forgot to tell you—" Realizing she'd stumbled over his words again, she stopped with a grimace. "You go ahead."

"No. What were you saying?"

"Just that I forgot to tell you I'll be out of town this weekend. I'm going home to Russellville for a couple days to see my parents. I figure I'd better see them before we start the surgery rotation, because there won't be much time while we're on that block. I won't get to see them again until Thanksgiving."

He waited for a moment, but the invitation he half expected didn't materialize. He wasn't sure if he was relieved or disappointed. He supposed they hadn't reached the spend-time-with-the-parents stage. He knew he certainly wasn't ready to inflict his family on Haley yet, though for totally different reasons.

"You, um, have told your parents that you and I are more than study buddies now, haven't you?" he asked, surveying her face closely.

Her eyes met his then skidded away. "Not exactly. I really don't discuss my sex life with my parents."

Sex life. He didn't really like that phrase. Sure, he and Haley were lovers, but it was somewhat more than that. Right?

Maybe he needed to remind himself why there was little chance he and Haley were meant to be together forever.

"Don't think I'll be seeing my family anytime soon," he said casually. "They're all pretty scattered."

She sank into the armchair, studying him curiously. "You'll go home for the holidays, won't you? Thanksgiving or Christmas?"

"Probably not Thanksgiving. Maybe a day or two during Christmas break."

He had spent last Thanksgiving watching football and studying alone in his apartment. Because none of his siblings had gone home for the holiday, he'd claimed a need to study to avoid doing so, himself. Cowardice, maybe, but he hadn't wanted to subject himself to his father's distance and his mother's criticism at that time.

Last year had been so very difficult. He'd been overwhelmed by the sheer volume of the material he'd been expected to memorize, by the number and frequency of the tests on that material, not to mention the clinical lessons and preparations for the looming Step 1 of the licensure exam. He just couldn't face his parents and their open skepticism that he'd ever make it all the way through to obtaining his M.D. He'd had too many doubts, himself, at the time. Had it not been for his friends, he might well have given up.

By not telling his study friends he had no other plans for Thanksgiving last year, he hadn't had to deal with invitations to spend the holidays with their families, which always made him feel awkward and out of place. He would be just as content to spend the upcoming holiday quietly on his own, for that matter. He'd gone home to northeastern Arkansas both of the past two Christmases, but hadn't particularly enjoyed the visits and had come back to Little Rock after only a few hours with his difficult family.

Haley looked as disapproving as he'd expected. "You should at least spend a little time during the holidays with your family if you want to mend fences with them."

After some of the things she'd already seen on the wards, he'd think she'd be a little less rosy-eyed about families. He supposed the more time she spent with some of the more questionable elements of society, the more cynical she would become. A shame, really, but probably necessary if she was going to succeed in her chosen field.

"I'm not entirely sure I do want to mend those fences," he said gently. "Not every family unit is worth saving."

Haley sighed a little and shook her head. "I don't believe in giving up."

He laughed softly, grabbed her wrist and tugged her down on the couch beside him. "I know. You've been saying that to me for two and a half years."

Steadying herself with a hand against his chest, she laughed ruefully. "Sorry. It just slipped out."

"No need to apologize. I'm glad you're the type who never gives up." Especially on him, he added silently as his lips covered hers.

She wrapped her arms around his neck, snuggling closer for the very thorough kiss. After a few long, delectable moments, she squirmed as if in discomfort, and he loosened his grasp.

Pulling her mouth from his, she glanced downward, then looked up with a smile that made his heart stutter.

"I have always wanted to say this," she said, trying to keep a straight face. "Is that a gun in your pocket or—"

"—I am very happy to see you," he said with a laugh, swooping in for another kiss.

Relieved to put thoughts of families and holidays aside, he laughed with her as they worked together to extricate him from the holster, their hands fumbling, then lingering. There was plenty of time for serious talk later. For now, he was just going to enjoy.

Haley discovered quickly that the surgery rotation was as exhausting as Anne had warned.

Out of the four choices Haley had been given—trauma, surgical oncology, VA and peds—she had marked trauma as her first choice, thinking she would see the biggest variety and learn the most on that block. Ron had selected surgical oncology as his first choice. Which didn't surprise her, really. She had noticed his fascination with hematology and oncology, though he hadn't openly declared that was the specialty he wanted to pursue. Specifically, she thought he was interested in pediatrics hem-onc.

Why wouldn't he just admit it? Was he afraid to say what he really wanted, in case he didn't get it? Or was he just hesitant to commit himself to any specific path at this point?

Shouldn't she know him well enough to have those answers by now?

They'd both gotten their first choices, so the surgeries they witnessed were quite different, though their schedules were very similar.

Wearing scrubs, Haley arrived at the hospital before five every morning to see her assigned patients. Between six and six-thirty, she went on rounds with the resident and attending surgeon. Between seven and seven-thirty, she scrubbed in for surgeries. The scrubbing was a lengthy and meticulous process, after which she had to hold her gloved hands above her belly button line. If she dropped her hands below that zone, she was no longer sterile and had to rescrub. It was so easy to let her hands fall accidentally; she had to pay a lot of attention to their placement, though she was assured it would come more naturally with practice.

During the surgeries, she served as second assistant. The resident was first assistant. As a student, Haley was allowed to hold the retractors and occasionally hand an instrument to the Registered Nurse. With the surgeon, resident, R.N. and scrub tech surrounding the patient, not counting the anesthesiologist at the patient's head, the student had the worst view of the entire procedure, but Haley was still fascinated by it all. Sometimes after a routine surgery, the attending surgeon would leave the resident to close, and Haley became first assistant. Her resident was quite nice, and allowed Haley to tie a few sutures, which was especially exciting for her.

After surgeries, she checked on her patients again and did afternoon rounds. Sometimes there were afternoon surgeries to scrub in on. She was also expected to see her patients on weekends. Once a week, there were grand rounds, at which she had to dress in professional clothing and her white coat rather than the comfortable scrubs.

Though the med students put in long hours on this rotation, surgical residents practically lived at the hospital, putting in eighty hours a week and having to rush to get all their responsibilities crammed into that legally mandated time frame. She'd lucked out on her resident again. Mike Stanfield was a pleasant, second-year resident who hadn't yet allowed himself to adopt the all-too-common surgeon's egotism. He was as susceptible to a surgical resident's exhaustion and stress as his peers, but he wasn't as prone as some to take out his problems on the staff and students surrounding him.

Ron hadn't been as fortunate. His resident, Paul Singer, was a...well, a jerk was the only description that came to Haley's mind when she thought of him. Arrogant, intoxicated with what he saw as the power of his long white coat, abusive to anyone he considered his inferior—which were most of the people around him, including the patients. He made no secret of the fact that he'd chosen medicine primarily because he liked the salary potential, and surgery because he didn't have to spend a lot of time with conscious patients. Like the other surgical residents, he was overworked and under-rested, but he directed his anger toward the nurses and med students.

Singer particularly disliked Ron, because Ron made no pretense of being either impressed by him or intimidated by him. He treated Singer with the same easy manner as he did everyone else, giving him the professional courtesy he deserved, but refusing to be browbeaten by him.

"The guy has it in for me," Ron admitted to Haley after one particularly rough day. "He deliberately bumped into me and made me break the sterile field to steady myself, then yelled at me for being an idiot and not knowing how to stand in an

O.R.. This after he dropped a retractor and blamed the scrub tech for it. Doing everything he could to make everyone else look like idiots in front of the attending."

"Jerk." Haley nestled more snugly into his shoulder on her couch, offering comfort with a hug. "What did the attending do?"

Ron shrugged. "Dr. Rankin pretty much ignores him. Either she's just used to the guy or she doesn't really care how he acts. I can't get a handle on what she's thinking. She doesn't say much. Just does the cutting, barks out instructions, then leaves Paul to close up and abuse the help. She's not outright rude to anyone, the way Singer is, but she's not overly friendly, either. I'll just be glad when I'm off this team."

"I don't blame you."

"I'll probably get crappy evals from them, especially since Singer hates me. No telling what he's saying about me to Rankin behind my back."

"I hope it won't be too bad. As hard as it must be, you need to try to get along with Singer while you're on his team."

"I'm not the one being a jackass," Ron answered flatly. "I'll do my job, but I won't kiss up to the idiot. But I'll also try not to take a swing at him, the way I hear one nurse did recently."

She winced. "Male or female nurse?"

"A woman. Almost flattened the twerp. Of course, she was suspended. I heard he was told to be nicer to the staff, but since there was no real consequence to his behavior, he paid no attention."

"I hate to think he's going to be treating patients."

"Yeah. Treating them like garbage. But there's nothing we can do about it."

"You should report his behavior to someone. Surely someone cares that he's acting that way."

"Honey, he's probably been reported a million times. No one cares as long as he keeps doing the job. Which he does. The lousy thing is, he's a good surgeon. Might even be great one day if no one breaks his fingers first."

"Talent is no excuse to treat other people with so much disrespect. My resident's a good surgeon, too, but he's decent to people. I've only heard him snap a few times, usually when it was warranted, and always followed by an apology when it wasn't justified."

"Yeah, Singer would probably choke before he'd get an apology out. Which wouldn't be such a bad thing, considering." Ron dropped a kiss on top of her head, then said lightly, "Oh, well, just two more weeks on this team and then I can move on to the next block. If I get lousy evaluations, whatever. I don't want to go into surgery, anyway."

She frowned, still suspecting he was interested in pursuing hematology and oncology. "You're going to just let them say whatever they want about you without even trying to defend yourself?"

"No get-in-there-and-fight lectures tonight, okay, Haley? I'm just too tired for a locker-room talk right now."

She straightened abruptly away from him. "I'm only trying to help. What if Singer's spitefulness somehow does cause you problems in the future?"

"Then I'll deal with it. Don't worry so much about it."

"Just try to get along with him, okay?"

He lifted an eyebrow. "I'll handle it."

He was starting to sound annoyed, and she bit back any more expressions of concern that he seemed to be so nonchalant about the possibility that his unpleasant resident would hurt his résumé. Maybe he was right, maybe one ill-tempered resident and one uncaring attending wouldn't cause much trouble for Ron. But that didn't mean he should just give up and say there was nothing he could do about it.

Irked with him for not listening to her, she shrugged. "Fine. It's your career."

"Exactly."

Scowling, she pushed herself off the couch and stalked toward the kitchen to pour herself a cup of coffee. She intended to spend the rest of the evening studying. If Ron wanted to join her, fine. If not—that was his business, too.

Chapter Eight

Maybe it was because Ron was having such a difficult time in his rotation, but Haley sensed a new distance between them as the long Thanksgiving weekend approached. It was a tough rotation for both of them. The hours were long and the work demanding. They didn't even try to spend much time together during those weeks. It was simply easier when they weren't working to go to their individual apartments and get as much rest as possible, taking every free waking moment as an opportunity to study and prepare for the following day.

Maybe Ron's tension had nothing at all to do with her, Haley tried to reassure herself. Maybe it was due to his problems with his resident and his concerns about doing well in the challenging rotation. Maybe he was just tired.

He certainly looked exhausted on the Tuesday before Thanksgiving when they managed to grab an hour to have lunch together in the hospital cafeteria. They'd talked shop during the meal, staying away from personal issues in such a public venue. At least, the conversation didn't get personal until Ron indirectly brought up the looming holiday, a topic they had yet to discuss.

"At least we'll have a couple days off after tomorrow," he muttered, wearily massaging the back of his neck with one hand as he pushed his empty soup bowl away with the other. "I plan to sleep for at least ten straight hours, if I can manage it. And after that, I won't have to work with Singer ever again, if I'm lucky."

She frowned. "You are going home for Thanksgiving, aren't you?"

She had simply assumed that he would dine with his family that day, as she would with her own. It didn't seem odd to her that neither had extended an invitation to the other; their relationship was hardly at the spend-holidays-with-the-families stage.

But he shook his head with a slight shrug. "My family never made a big deal out of Thanksgiving. Dad's always at his deer camp that whole long weekend. He doesn't expect me to join him. He knows I've never been much of a hunter— just one of many disappointments for him when it comes to me."

"What about your mother?"

"She goes to her sister's house for Thanksgiving. My aunt Belinda, who can't stand my dad and isn't too crazy about any of the rest of us. She's been warming up to me a little since I started medical school—she likes the idea of having a doctor nephew—but let's just say I'd prefer to keep our relationship the way it's always been. A distant one."

She moistened her lips. "So what are you going to do for Thanksgiving?"

His smile was probably intended to be reassuring. "I just told you. I'm going to sleep in, watch some football, maybe order a pizza. And for one entire day, I'm not even going to open a medical textbook. It'll be great."

She struggled internally while she gathered her dishes. And then the words tumbled out of her. "Why don't you join my family for Thanksgiving dinner? I'm sure my parents would be delighted to have you."

He shot her a look across the small table. "Thanks, Haley, but I'll be fine on my own. Really."

He thought she had extended the invitation out of pity—and she supposed he was right, for the most part. It wasn't that she didn't want to spend the day with Ron—but she had to admit to herself that it worried her a bit to include him in her family holiday. She would analyze the reason for that later.

"I'm sure you will be fine," she said with a breezy smile. "But I'll be in the car almost two and a half hours that day, round-trip. I would enjoy the company."

He studied her face very closely, making her resist shifting self-consciously in her seat. "Do you want me to come with you?"

"I wouldn't have asked if I didn't want you to—"

"Haley," he cut in firmly, his eyes holding hers. "Do you want me to be with you on Thanksgiving?"

There was a lot more to that seemingly simple question than was immediately apparent. More for her to evaluate later, she decided, keeping her response strictly on the surface. "I would love for you to join us. As I said, it would be nice to have company for the drive."

He frowned, and she could tell he wasn't satisfied with her tone. He seemed to want something more from her— something she couldn't quite decipher in this time and place. Did he want her to assure him that he meant much more to her than a temporary bedmate—or to reassure him that she wasn't expecting anything more?

She didn't have time to fret about it now. And this certainly wasn't the place for an intimate conversation, she thought as someone bumped her shoulder with a tray, moving on without even an apology.

She glanced at her watch. "I have to get back upstairs. Let's consider this settled, shall we? You're joining us for Thanksgiving."

"It wouldn't do any good for me to argue with you, would it?"

"None at all." With a nod, she stood and picked up her tray. After only a momentary hesitation, Ron followed suit.

No holiday had ever been more welcome to Haley. She desperately needed the four days off, even though she expected to spend a good portion of that time studying.

She'd learned so much during the past month, she thought wearily early Thanksgiving morning as she sat behind the wheel of her car, headed toward her family home in Russellville. She was looking forward to doing her second month of surgery rotation, which would be divided into two, two-week blocks.

She glanced at the passenger riding quietly in the other seat, gazing out the window at the scenery they passed along westbound Interstate 40. She still wondered if she'd done the right thing by persuading Ron to join her today, even though his first instinct had apparently been to politely decline.

It wasn't that she hadn't wanted him to come along, she assured herself. It was only that there was so much potential for awkwardness with her family. Her parents hadn't thought it at all odd when she'd told them that she'd invited Ron. But they still thought he was just one of her study friends. Would they be able to tell the difference in the relationship once they saw her and Ron together?

They'd been lovers for almost two months now, though they had spent only a few nights together. The fact that they didn't spend even more time together was partially due to their busy schedules, but also a deliberate choice on her part. She didn't want Ron leaving his toothbrush at her place or hanging his shirts in her closet. That was no way to keep their relationship breezy and casual and fun. Getting too intimately entwined was a sure way to end up with a hole in her life—and another in her heart. She was relieved that she hadn't had to spell out her conditions to him; he seemed to understand the boundaries she'd implicitly drawn, and he had never overstepped them.

Probably because he was as determined as she was to keep this all light and easy, she thought, remembering how skittish Ron had always been about commitments. She suspected that was part of the reason he'd been so hesitant to accept her Thanksgiving invitation; spending time with the family probably skirted a bit too closely to long-term relationship territory for his comfort.

They'd settled into a routine that suited them both. They got together a couple of nights a week to study, share a meal, talk and laugh. And, occasionally, to share amazing, mind-blowing sex.

What they did not do was talk about the future. Or share any deep emotions. There were still many things Ron had not told her about his past—nor did he seem inclined to do so. Which was one of the clues, as far as she was concerned, that he was no more thinking permanence than she was.

They were having fun. Enjoying each other. Relieving some of the stress of medical school by playing. No need to add to the stress they were already under by trying to force a relationship neither of them was ready for, she assured herself.

"You're quiet today," she commented, needing a distraction from her line of thinking.

He turned toward her with a smile. "Just enjoying the ride. Feels good to be out of the hospital for a day, doesn't it?"

"I was just thinking that. I know you're glad to have that rotation behind you."

"Yeah. No more Singer. Hooray."

She smiled. "So has he completely destroyed your former interest in hem-onc?"

"I was never interested in surgery," he replied lightly. "I kind of like having a life outside the hospital."

Which hadn't exactly answered her question. "So hem-onc is still on the table for your specialty?"

"Depends on which residency program I can charm my way into," he quipped with a laugh.

She wasn't amused. "You can get into any residency program you want, Ron."

"Hmm." With that vague, inscrutable murmur, he turned to look out the window again. And she let him get away with it because thoughts of residency programs, quite probably in different states, depressed her a little. That was no way to feel on Thanksgiving.

Ten more miles passed in silence. They passed the town of Conway, about halfway to Russellville. Wondering why he was being so uncharacteristically quiet, she asked curiously, "Are you nervous about meeting my parents?"

He looked at her with lifted brows. "I've met your parents before."

"Well, yes, in passing, with the rest of the study group. But this is a little different."

"Because it's only me this time, you mean?"

"Well, that and…you know."

"Because I'm sleeping with their daughter now?"

She nodded wryly. "I guess that's what I meant."

"I wasn't sure you'd told them that part."

"I haven't," she said quickly, her eyes on the road ahead. "That's not the sort of thing you tell your parents."

"But you have told them we're seeing each other now, haven't you? As more than study friends, I mean."

"My parents know we're very good friends."

He turned in his seat, shifting his seat belt to let him consider her more fully. "You haven't told them?"

"Like I said, there are some things they don't need to know. I tell my mom when we do things—like when we went to the fair and to the Halloween party—so she knows we spend a lot of time together."

"But they think we're still just friends."

"Very good friends," she said again, a little wary of his tone.

Why did he sound so aggrieved? She would think he'd be relieved that she hadn't made an issue of their changed relationship. Seemed to her as though that would take some of the pressure off him as far as spending time with her parents. He wouldn't have to wonder if they were assessing him as a potential son-in-law. That just wasn't an issue between her and Ron.

He shrugged. "I guess you know best what to say to your folks. You know I've never been close to my own, so I don't tell them much of anything about my life, but I thought it was different with you and your parents. Thought you'd tell them we're a couple now."

A couple. Her fingers tightened on the steering wheel. She was sure he hadn't meant that the way it sounded, but still...

"Yes, well, I don't tell them everything."

"So, you don't want me to make an issue of it?"

She shrugged, keeping her gaze firmly fixed ahead. "You know. Parents worry. They'd probably fret about whether I'm staying focused on my training, whether I'm getting enough rest, that sort of thing."

"So as far as they're concerned, we are still just friends."

"Very good friends." She didn't know why she kept stressing that, as though it were a boon to his ego or something, but he didn't comment. Only turned his attention out the window again.

They'd passed Morrilton and were almost to Russellville when he spoke again, surprising her with his topic. "My family's getting together the weekend before Christmas this year. Mom called yesterday to tell me about it. She said it was the only time everyone could get together."

"So they're having the family Christmas gathering early."

"Yeah, by a few days. My sister's bringing her boys from Florida to see their grandparents—and get their presents, of course. Mom wants everyone to come while Deb's there."

It was the first time he'd even mentioned his sister's name. "Your whole family will be there?"

"Well, except my brother Tommy. He's not eligible for parole for a couple years yet."

She still didn't know what his brother had done to be incarcerated, but she figured that was none of her business, so she didn't ask. "What about your other brother?"

"Yeah, Mom said Mick was going to try to make it. It's off-season for carnies, so he'll probably be able to take a few days."

"And you'll be there, of course."

"Not sure. I told her I didn't know what my schedule would be that weekend."

"You should be able to take that one weekend off. You'll be almost done with your surgery rotation."

"I'll need to be studying for the surgery shelf exam."

"You can spend extra time before and after studying. Your family is reaching out to you, Ron. Shouldn't you at least make the effort?"

His short laugh held little humor. "Trust me, it's not going to be a Rockwell family reunion. Dad will drink the whole weekend, same as he always does. He gets quietly smashed, then just sits and stares at the TV, throwing an occasional insult around. Mom will bitch about how no one ever comes to visit, and then about how much work it is for her when we do. Mick will do some drinking, then he and Dad will get into it over something and Mick'll storm off. And at some point during all that, Deb will burst into tears and rush out of the room."

"And you?" she asked, inwardly cringing at the dispassionate prediction.

"I'll crack some jokes. Sometimes the others will laugh, other times they'll get ticked off, but that's what they expect from their youngest kid."

"You should go."

"Oh, yeah, sounds like a riot, doesn't it?"

"Seriously, Ron. You should go see your family. It will never get any better between you if you don't even try."

After a moment, he nodded. "I'll go—if you'll go with me."

"Um—me?"

"I'm going with you to your family gathering," he reminded her.

Well, yes—but she wasn't asking him to serve as a barrier between her and her family. "You don't think it would be awkward to have me there?"

He shrugged. "No more awkward than it ever is. And maybe they'll behave a little better if we have a guest."

"I haven't even been invited."

"I told Mom I might bring my girlfriend. She said you'd be welcome."

His girlfriend. The term made her swallow, but then she told herself it had probably been the easiest way to define their relationship to his mother. She supposed it was true enough. For now.

She had to admit she was curious about Ron's family. She would like to see the people who'd shaped him, who'd made him the man he was now. She found it hard to believe they were quite as bad as he implied, since he'd turned out so well.

"All right," she said, turning on her blinker to signal her upcoming exit from the freeway toward her parents' house. "I'll go with you."

"You will?"

"Sure. I'd like to meet your family."

"No. Trust me. You won't like it."

She rolled her eyes. "I still want to meet them."

"Okay, fine. If I decide to go, I'll take you with me. Be prepared for a lot of hours on the road that day, because if I go, I'll leave early Saturday, make the three hour drive, stay a few hours, then head back. I have neither the time nor interest in spending the night."

Six hours in a car seemed like a rather stiff price for satisfying her curiosity about him, but she'd already committed now. She didn't go back on her word. "Okay, then. We'll bring materials and study in the car together during the ride."

"No time wasted, huh?"

She smiled in response to his wry drawl. "No more than necessary."

"That's my Haley."

Turning into the driveway of her parents' modest, three-bedroom, redbrick ranch house, she told herself it was only a figure of speech, not a declaration. But hearing him call her "his" Haley still elicited a funny little flutter from somewhere in the pit of her stomach.

If Haley really thought her parents weren't aware that something had changed, she was deluding herself, Ron decided midway through the Thanksgiving meal. He could tell from the moment her parents greeted him in the living room that they were eyeing him differently than they had before. Maybe her mother had heard something in Haley's voice when she'd talked about their recent adventures together; maybe they just knew their daughter better than she suspected. But they knew.

He couldn't tell if they approved. They didn't seem to disapprove, exactly. They were certainly warm and welcoming to him, seemed genuinely pleased to have him join them for the holiday meal. Janice seemed delighted with the big bouquet of fall flowers he'd brought as a hostess gift. But they watched him, and he thought he saw a sizing up in those glances, especially from her father.

Her aunt and uncle, Noelle and Victor Wright, joined them for the meal. Janice and Russell, Haley's parents, seemed delighted to serve as hosts, even though they performed that same service seven days a week at their restaurant. Haley had taken the whole study group to Pasta Wright to celebrate the successful ending of their first year of classes, and her parents had pulled out all the stops, feeding them an amazing four-course Italian feast and refusing to allow them to pay a cent.

This meal was just as delicious, though the dishes were traditional American Thanksgiving fare. The conversation around the beautifully decorated table was lively and amusing, the affection in the dining room palpable. There was a brief, spirited debate between brothers Russell and Victor over some issue in local politics, but it ended with laughter and good-natured insults. It would have ended much differently for Ron's family.

He'd been around other functional families, of course. He'd spent a lot of time hanging out with his high school best friend's big, rowdy, supportive clan, then during his first two years of college had dated a young woman from a great family he still considered friends. He was even godfather to his ex-girlfriend's first child, which said something about what a nice guy she'd married three years ago. So he was under no illusion that all families were as messed up as his own. For that matter, he knew there were families much worse than the one he'd been born into.

It was just nice to be reminded occasionally how pleasant a family meal could be.

"So, what type of medicine are you planning to practice, Ron?" Victor asked over dessert.

Ron swallowed a bite of the creamiest pumpkin pie he'd ever tasted and dabbed at his mouth with a linen napkin. Lulled by the delicious meal and friendly atmosphere, he replied candidly, "I'm thinking pedi hem-onc. Sorry. Pediatric hematology and oncology."

He was aware of Haley's quick look of surprise. He supposed she knew he was intrigued by the specialty, but it was the first time he'd specifically said so. He didn't know why, exactly, he'd been so reluctant to discuss his future plans with her.

"Oncology. That's cancer, isn't it?" her aunt Noelle asked with a slight frown. "Children's cancer?"

He nodded. "Yes, ma'am. I did a rotation in the pedi hem-onc ward, and I've just come off a surgical oncology rotation. I find it all very interesting."

The older woman shook her blond-highlighted head slowly. "I don't think I could handle that. Too sad."

"It is sad when children are afflicted with cancer," he answered patiently. "But because of modern medical treatment, the overall survival rate for all the types of pediatric cancer is nearly eighty percent. It's more than eighty-seven percent for lymphoblastic leukemia, which is the most common form of childhood cancer."

"That high?" Russell looked surprised. "That is an encouraging number, isn't it?"

"Yes, it is. It depends on the type and progression of the cancer, of course."

"Is pedi hem-onc a difficult residency to get into?" Russell asked, somewhat self-consciously using the medical jargon.

Ron shrugged. "Harder than some, easier than others. If I don't get accepted into one, I'll just fall back on Plan B."

Janice frowned. "I'm sure you'll get into any program you want. You should keep a positive attitude."

He smothered a smile, deliberately not looking at Haley. So this was where she got her cheerleader attitude. "Yes, ma'am. I'll do that."

"Are you still thinking about psychiatry, Haley?"

"Yes, Aunt Noelle, that's still my plan. I'll do a psychiatry rotation next semester, and I'll probably know for certain after that."

"Will you and Ron both be able to stay in Little Rock for your residencies?"

Ron glanced sideways at Haley, noting her sudden frown with a sinking feeling. True, they hadn't discussed that far ahead, but did she have to look quite so unnerved by the possibility that they'd be interviewing for residency programs in the same places? He supposed he should reassure her at some point that he wouldn't expect her to make any career compromises for him. She was perfectly free to apply anywhere she wanted, just as he supposed he would do, himself.

"Ron and I will make whatever choices are best for our futures, Aunt Noelle. Mom, is there any more coffee or should I make another pot?"

Maybe the others took the hint that she didn't want to talk about the future, or maybe they were just ready to move on to another topic. More coffee was served all around, after which everyone moved to the den to chat and play a couple of board games while college football played on the large screen TV. Ron threw himself fully into the activities, making a special effort to be a polite and amusing guest. He was rewarded with laughter from all of them, even Haley.

Yet, deep inside he continued to be bothered by the feeling that something was going on between him and Haley that he didn't fully understand.

* * *

The second month of the surgery rotation consisted of two, two-week blocks. Haley had selected burn and transplant as her choices; Ron had opted for plastics and vascular surgery. While she knew burn surgeries would be difficult to witness, Haley thought there was much to learn in that specialty. Transplants also intrigued her. She assumed Ron had similar reasons for making his choices.

Her schedule now was as hectic as it had been during the first month of surgery. Once again she had to be at the hospital before dawn. By the time she dragged home hours later, she was exhausted from being on her feet all day. The surgeries lasted for hours, and the O.R.'s were kept extremely warm to preserve the patients' body heat. The patients were very sick, which meant there was a lot of tension in the room, the constant threat of the patients coding.

She was able to do quite a few things in that rotation, including assisting with skin grafts. She was proud of herself for handling the sights and the pressure; only once did she have to step out for a moment when the heat made her a little light-headed. She followed recommendations she'd learned during the first month of surgery to keep her knees unlocked and to make sure she kept her blood sugar up by having a good breakfast and occasional protein breaks. Both helped her endure the long procedures.

Because of their hours and because they were assigned to different hospitals, she and Ron didn't see much of each other during those two weeks. It bothered her how badly she missed him even during that brief, busy separation.

It was ridiculous to feel that way, she chided herself. They had their own lives, their own interests, their own paths ahead. She predicted fast-paced, fulfilling careers for each of them.

Whatever direction their individual choices took them, she hoped they would always remain friends. She couldn't bear the thought of a future that didn't include Ron in some way.

Oddly enough, it was the fear of losing his friendship that made her push him away after Thanksgiving. She was aware of what she was doing, but she couldn't seem to stop herself. The more heated their physical relationship became, the more she worried that the inevitable end would be explosive. Painful. Making it impossible for them to maintain any sort of friendly connection afterward.

She couldn't say she regretted that she and Ron had given in to the attraction that had simmered between them from the start. In hindsight, it seemed inevitable that they would end up in bed together. Maybe it was as certain that their parting would be as volatile as their friendship had always been. But just the thought of a bitter split made her heart ache. She felt helpless to stop it, paralyzed by indecision—and ruefully aware that her apprehension was leading to the very outcome she dreaded.

Ron called when he had free time, and they talked easily enough, sharing stories about their days. But each time he suggested they get together for dinner or a movie or just to spend a little time with each other, she demurred, telling him that she was simply too busy or too tired or too overwhelmed with studying and preparations for the next day's demands. She sensed he was growing annoyed with her excuses, but he didn't push for explanations, to her relief.

Compounding her many responsibilities, the class holiday party was scheduled for the second weekend in December, the Saturday before Ron was expected for his family's Christmas gathering. Because she was expected to arrive early to help with the decorations and preparations, she told Ron that she'd take her own car to the country club where the party was being held. He agreed, though he sounded a little cool and grumpy when they ended that phone call shortly afterward.

Tossing her phone aside, Haley sank into the cushions of her sofa in her quiet, lonely apartment, sadly wondering if the affair had already ended because of her cowardly machinations. And wistfully hoping that she and Ron could somehow find their way back to friendship if it had.

Though she arrived at the country club more than an hour before the party was supposed to begin, there was barely time to complete all the preparations. She and Anne, who'd volunteered to help, surreptitiously high-fived when they finished just as the first guests began to wander in.

There hadn't been time for chitchat while they'd worked, but they could relax now as they both accepted a glass of wine from a smiling server.

"Have I told you how nice you look tonight?" Anne asked, motioning with her wineglass toward Haley's sleek, floor-length black dress. "I haven't seen that gown before."

"I found it on a clearance rack last weekend," Haley confessed with a laugh. "I realized sort of at the last minute that I had nothing to wear to a dress-up affair."

Anne looked beautiful in a long, silvery-blue dress that complemented her blond hair and fair skin, and Haley told her so. "It's a shame Liam isn't here to admire you."

Liam roamed around the globe for the adventure travel program he hosted on cable television. Haley never knew where he was when he wasn't in Little Rock with his wife.

Anne sighed. "He's in Kuala Lumpur. But he promised he'd be home in time for Christmas."

"Glad to hear that."

Anne glanced around the rapidly filling room, waving to acknowledge a greeting before asking, "Where's Ron?"

Haley glanced at her watch with a frown. "I guess he's running late. I thought he'd be here by now."

"How's he been? I haven't seen him since before Thanksgiving."

"He's fine, though he and I haven't had time to see each other much during the past two weeks, either. I talked to him last night, though. He's enjoyed plastics. He said he had a cool resident who let him do a lot. The reconstructive part of plastic surgery appealed to Ron; he liked seeing what they can do to make the patients stop dreading looking into a mirror."

"That sounds like Ron. He really is a marshmallow, isn't he?"

"Yes, I suppose he is. Especially when it comes to kids. He has a gooey center in that respect."

"He'll be a great dad someday."

Haley swallowed in response to the seemingly out-of-the-blue comment. Thinking of Ron as a father gave her a funny feeling deep inside her chest, a combination of sadness and longing. She'd always imagined herself having children someday. There was still that tricky double standard in medicine, as in so many careers, which made it more difficult for women than for men to take time to have families, but she knew it was possible.

As for Ron—he had trouble fully committing even to a career path, always wanting to leave his options open in case he changed his mind. She doubted he would be eager to take on the lifelong responsibilities of parenthood.

"Maybe someday."

Had Anne been hinting when she'd said that Ron would make a good father? Probably. After her initial reservations, Anne seemed to have concluded that Haley and Ron made a good couple. Being blissfully married herself, still practically in the honeymoon stage, she could be forgiven for wanting the same happiness for her friends. But Haley and Ron? Surely Anne could see how unlikely that imagined happily-ever-after would be.

A woman prone to giving too much of herself and a man who held too much back? Heartbreak in the making.

Haley knew how to make commitments, but she had always maintained a healthy dose of self-preservation. She dedicated herself fully to a cause only when she truly believed a positive outcome was achievable.

The success of her family's new restaurant venture back when she was in high school? Achievable, and she'd thrown herself into helping them. Earning her undergraduate degree, doing well on the MCAT, getting into medical school? All achievable. Keeping her grades high and her test scores respectable during her training? Tough, but achievable. Getting into a good residency program, maybe even a triple-board program if she chose to go that route? Also achievable, if she stayed on her current course.

Maintaining a lifelong relationship with a fellow student who wouldn't even commit to a first choice of a specialty? Who had once mentioned to the group that he'd never been involved in a serious, long-term relationship with a woman? Who even seemed willing to give up on his own family because of their shortcomings?

She might be an optimist, but she wasn't a masochist.

She was relieved when two classmates Kristie and Lydia, in sparkling holiday dresses, wandered up to chat with her and Anne, bringing an end to that suddenly uncomfortable conversation. Or so she had hoped. After only a brief exchange of small talk, one of the newcomers looked at Haley curiously.

"Where's Ron? He's coming tonight, isn't he?"

Haley smiled brightly. "Yes, he said he'd be here. I guess he's just running a little late. You know Ron."

Kristie laughed. "Without you there to keep him on track, he's probably been distracted by a video game or something."

Lydia grinned. "Or gotten into a conversation with somebody he passed in a hallway or parking lot. You know how Ron loves to talk and clown around."

"And flirt," Kristie agreed with an arched look at Haley. "Does that ever bother you, Haley? The way he flirts and teases with all the women around him?"

She lifted an eyebrow. "Why would it bother me? Ron's just very friendly—he flirts with his senior citizen patients as much as he does with women our age."

"You don't worry that someone else might decide to flirt back?"

Haley shrugged lightly. "No. I don't worry about that. Ron and I don't have that sort of relationship."

Lydia frowned. "I thought you were dating. I mean, you're together almost all the time at parties and everything."

"We've dated, but it's nothing serious," Haley said. She didn't know if she was trying to convince them or herself—or why she felt the need to do either at that moment. Maybe she was simply trying to save face if it turned out that Ron had already decided this complicated affair wasn't worth the effort. "I have no claim on Ron if he wants to go out with someone else."

"Oh. Well."

Kristie and Lydia exchanged looks as if they didn't know what to say. Haley was aware that Anne was studying her with a frown, but she studiously avoided her friend's eyes.

"I guess I thought you and Ron had more of a commitment," Lydia commented with a shrug and a quizzical smile.

Haley gave a little laugh that sounded fake even to her. "After two and a half years, you should know Ron better than that, Lydia. He doesn't do commitment."

Kristie blinked, then looked past Haley's shoulder. "Oh. Speak of the devil."

Haley whirled. How did he keep doing this?

Ron was in midstep toward her, far enough away that she wasn't quite sure whether he was close enough to have heard anything they said. She certainly couldn't tell by his expression, which was as relaxed and cheery as usual. Like everyone else, he had dressed for the occasion, and he looked delicious in his dark suit and white shirt. The tie he'd chosen was typically Ron—dark green festooned with a cartoon Santa Claus and flying, skipping and dancing reindeer.

"Don't you ladies look lovely tonight," he said in greeting, sharing an admiring smile with all of them equally.

"It's a nice change from scrubs," Lydia replied, her own smile coy as she glanced from Haley to Ron. "I was just standing here wishing someone would ask me to dance."

Ron gave a little bow. "Well, far be it from me to let a pretty lady be disappointed. Shall we?"

Giggling, Lydia placed a hand on his arm. "Sure."

Glancing over his shoulder, Ron spoke to Haley. "I'll catch up with you later, okay?"

Oh, yes, she thought with a hard swallow. He'd heard enough to tick him off but good, despite the lazy grin he wore for the others.

She turned to Anne when the others had moved away, only to find Anne looking at her with a frown of disapproval. Because she was in no mood for a lecture—even if she probably deserved one—she turned away again. "I'd better go check with the caterer to make sure everything's under control."

She could almost feel Anne's fixed frown on the back of her neck as she walked away, silently calling herself a litany of unflattering names.

Chapter Nine

The party was winding to a close when Ron led Haley to the dance floor for the first time. She had been very busy mingling and directing the festivities; he suspected she'd deliberately used her social responsibilities as an excuse to avoid a one-on-one with him.

She needn't have worried, he thought grumpily, taking her into his arms for the slow number that was just beginning. He wouldn't do or say anything in this public venue that would set their classmates' tongues to wagging. Unlike Haley, herself, who hadn't seemed to mind announcing publicly that she considered him just a temporary bedmate.

Okay, maybe she hadn't phrased it exactly that way. But the message had been clear enough. She wasn't looking for a future with him. Apparently all those hints from others about how hard it would be for her to get into a competitive residency program while shackled to him had made an impact on her. Or maybe she'd seen this as a temporary diversion from the start.

He hadn't been prepared for the bolt of pain that had shot through him when he'd overheard her breezily assuring their classmates that he was free to date whomever he wanted. She'd even tried to blame it on him. *He doesn't do commitment,* she'd joked.

So maybe he had avoided commitment like the plague in the past. And maybe he'd made a point of declaring that phobia to all his friends. Maybe Haley had good reason to believe he'd been amenable to a no-strings, fun-while-it-lasted fling.

Maybe he'd expected her to understand that this time it was different. With her, he'd wanted much more. He'd thought— hoped—she knew him well enough to understand that.

Apparently, he'd been wrong. And because he'd never been one to chase after a lost cause, he supposed he'd have to acknowledge that those vague, uncharacteristic daydreams he'd indulged in lately were just that. Fantasies. It was time for him to get back to reality and accept that he'd never been meant for happily-ever-after endings.

Which didn't mean he couldn't enjoy the time he had to spend with her, he reminded himself in a silent pep talk. It just required a minor adjustment of his expectations. He could relish the time with her without getting his jaded heart broken when it ended.

Probably.

"You're being very quiet," Haley said tentatively, peering up at him. "Are you enjoying the party?"

He glanced around the beautifully decorated ballroom, which was getting a bit rowdy now that the guests had made a big dent in the liberally spiked punch. "It's great. You outdid yourself tonight."

Though she looked pleased by the compliment, she shook her head. "I certainly didn't do it all by myself. I had lots of help."

"I'm sure you were the primary organizer. You usually are."

Her smile turned to a momentary frown. Had he sounded bitter? He hadn't intended to.

"Anyway, great job, Haley. They all seem to be enjoying themselves."

"Thank you."

She fell silent again as he led her into a couple of tight turns with the music.

"We've hardly had time to talk since you started burns and I've been on plastics," he said, trying to fill the uncomfortable lull. "Guess you'll be ready for the Christmas break to rest up a little before starting next semester."

"I know everyone's looking forward to having a whole week off."

He couldn't say he was particularly anticipating the holiday. Haley would be spending time with her family and he'd be spending time alone, for the most part. He certainly didn't want to spend any more time with his own family than necessary, considering how their interactions usually ended up.

Maybe he would use the time on his own to remind himself that he actually preferred it that way.

"I was thinking about that thing at my parents' house next weekend," he said on impulse. "Maybe we should just skip it, you know?"

She frowned again. "What do you mean? Why would we skip your family's Christmas gathering?"

"I just don't think you'd enjoy it. I mean, you'll be spending the next two weeks on transplants, and that's going to wear you out. You won't want to spend your Saturday listening to my folks fuss when you could be resting and getting ready for the shelf exam."

She shook her head firmly. "I told you that I'd go with you, and I meant it. Unless—" Looking suddenly uncertain, she asked, "Would you rather go without me? If you think my being there will make things more awkward between you and your family, I would certainly understand."

"Actually, I was thinking of skipping out, too. I'll be busy with vascular and it's not like anyone there would really care if I don't show."

She was shaking her head before he even finished speaking. "Ron, you've already told your mother that we'll be there. It would be rude to cancel at this late hour."

He couldn't help responding to her naive statement with a short laugh. "Rude? Sugar, my family doesn't know the meaning of the word."

The song ended and they broke apart. Glancing around at the classmates who were studying them not-so-subtly, apparently sensing a quarrel in the making, Haley grabbed Ron's arm and towed him out of the ballroom through a French door that led out onto a brick lanai. Surrounded by outdoor dining tables that had been covered for the winter, she turned to him, her breath hanging in the chilly December air when she spoke.

"You said you were going to keep a positive attitude about this visit. Your brother and sister are making the effort. You should, too."

He looked at her in exasperation. Her dress had only fluttery strips of fabric where there should be sleeves, so she was probably freezing. At least he was wearing a jacket. He shrugged out of it and wrapped it around her shoulders, knowing she wouldn't drop this until they'd gotten it settled.

He spoke rationally, hoping to convince her quickly. "They aren't making that big an effort. Deb's probably got some agenda behind this visit. She doesn't usually make efforts unless there's something in it for her."

"That's a very cynical comment."

He shrugged. "Let's just say it's based on experience."

"Still, if you want to mend fences with your family..."

He squeezed the back of his neck, feeling the cold seeping through his thin dress shirt. "Just give it a rest, will you, Haley? Not every family is as 'Hollywood perfect' as yours."

Her eyes narrowed.

He knew that expression. He'd pushed another button. He hadn't intended to snap at her, but considering the way the evening had gone so far, he was in no mood to deal with one of her upbeat lectures about how to fix his dysfunctional family whom she'd never even met.

She planted her hands on her hips, almost dislodging his jacket. She made a quick grab for it, clutching it angrily around her. "I have never once claimed that my family is perfect," she said, the words escaping her in irritated little breath clouds.

"You didn't have to. I just spent a near-perfect Thanksgiving with them, didn't I? If you think it's going to be like that at my family gathering, I'm afraid you're in for a big shock."

He didn't know exactly why he was suddenly regretting asking her to join him. Maybe he really was just trying to prepare her for the worst. Maybe he was genuinely concerned that his family would get into one of their cutting quarrels, which would especially embarrass him after that Norman Rockwell holiday he'd just spent with hers.

Maybe he worried that once she saw where he'd come from, she'd have even less interest in accompanying him to where he was going.

He knew better than to say any of that aloud, of course. He was fully aware that his ramblings didn't exactly make sense, even to him. Which didn't mean they didn't have some basis in fact.

He blamed himself for the impulsive invitation on the way to her parents' home. Had he waited until after the near-perfect Thanksgiving meal with her family, he never would have put himself into this position. Especially after hearing her declare that she didn't consider their relationship a particularly significant one, anyway.

She took a step forward and poked him in the chest, her eyes gleaming in the multicolored Christmas lights draped from the roof and looped around nearly every available surface. "You invited me to your family's Christmas gathering and I'm holding you to that invitation, is that clear? If I have to go just to make sure that you do, then that's the way it will be. I'm not going to let you give up on your own family without making at least one more effort to repair your relationship with them."

God, he adored her. Those words he would probably never say lodged painfully in his throat when he muttered, "Okay, fine. We'll go. But don't blame me if it's a disaster."

"I'll only blame you if you don't make an effort," she assured him, looking satisfied that she'd railroaded him into agreeing.

"Your lips are turning blue."

She tucked her hands into his coat pockets and nodded. "I'm ready to go back inside. Everyone's probably wondering what we're doing out here, anyway."

He caught her arm when she turned toward the door, and planted a long, hard kiss on her cold lips. "Just warming you up," he muttered when he released her. He'd certainly raised his own internal heat level.

Blinking rather dazedly up at him, she cleared her throat and turned again toward the door, looking very much like a woman who had just been thoroughly kissed. Which should stop any conjecture that they'd been out here quarreling, he thought as he followed her back inside.

They left from Haley's apartment early the following Saturday headed for the northeast Arkansas town of Hurleyville.

Haley had never been there before; Ron assured her that she hadn't missed much. With less than eight thousand residents, the town had been dying off ever since the mill had closed back in the '80s. Ron's father had been laid off from that mill; since then, he'd made his living mostly working on old cars in his backyard garage.

The weather was hardly auspicious for their visit. It was unseasonably warm for early December, the sky gray and overcast. Thunderstorms with the potential to turn severe were predicted for later in the day. The threat of tornadoes in December was unusual, but not unheard of in Arkansas. Haley crossed her fingers that the weather wouldn't take an ugly turn before she and Ron were safely back in Little Rock that evening.

Looking at the skies as they prepared to climb into the car, Ron suggested they cancel the trip because of the weather threat. She sighed at the obvious ploy and told him to get behind the wheel.

Hefting a sigh, he fastened himself into the driver's seat. "Just don't say I didn't warn you. And I'm not talking about the weather now."

They'd barely gotten out of the Little Rock city limits when she reached for her netbook to start quizzing him for the upcoming shelf exam. Ron groaned. "Already?"

She was loading the first page of sample questions. "This was the plan, remember? To use the commute time to study?"

She figured studying was a good way to avoid the uncomfortable silences that had fallen between them during the past week, ever since their confrontation outside the country club. They'd both been too busy at the hospital to get into any long conversations—or maybe they'd just used that as an excuse to avoid doing so. She knew she hadn't wanted to talk about whatever he might have overheard her saying to Anne and Lydia and Kristie, and maybe Ron was no more eager to discuss their relationship. Whatever it was.

He had obviously withdrawn from her since that night. Because he hadn't liked what he'd heard? Because he was annoyed with her for pushing him into this family visit? Or because he'd seized on a convenient opportunity to start drawing back from her before they got too deeply involved?

Had the visit with her family initiated the change? She couldn't remember, exactly, though she knew that had been when she'd started to pull away. When she had realized how important he could become to her if she wasn't careful, how crucial a part of her life he could become if she let him. Maybe that visit with her "Hollywood perfect" family, as he'd called them, had scared him, too, for reasons of his own. Reasons she was too cowardly to discuss with him, she admitted with a swallowed sigh.

"I'm tired of studying," he admitted.

She gave a short laugh. "Yeah, well, too bad. You still have a year and a half of med school, then a minimum of four years of residency, and then career-long ongoing education. If you didn't want to study, you should have stuck with your carnival job."

"Nah. That was too hard work. And every time some little kid turned big, puppy-dog eyes on me, I caved and gave the kid one of the big prizes. I ended up spending more than I made."

Even though he sounded as though he were joking, she wouldn't have been at all surprised to learn there was some truth in that tale. Leaving the netbook open in her lap, she looked curiously at him. "You don't talk about that time much. Those few years after you graduated high school, I mean."

He shrugged. "I went to college. Partied too hard. Dropped out before the first semester ended rather than wait to flunk out. Tried working on cars with my dad for a while, but that was a disaster. Let my brother talk me into hitting the carnival circuit with him. Another disaster. Tried a couple of other jobs around Hurleyville. Hated them. Went back to school because I couldn't think of anything else to do. You know the rest."

She tilted her head thoughtfully. "There was a theme in those various pursuits. Are you aware of it?"

He glanced at her with a quizzical smile. "A theme? What are you talking about?"

"You tried working with your father and your brother, and then taking jobs in your hometown. It sounds to me as if you were trying to maintain a bond with your family."

He frowned, looking startled by the suggestion as he turned his attention back to the road ahead. "That's not it. I was just looking for a way to support myself, and those were the first options that presented themselves to me. Like I said, they were all debacles."

But he'd tried. And despite whatever bitterness he carried from his childhood, he still hadn't cut off ties with his family. "Maybe things will get better in your family now that you're all out on your own. As long as you keep trying, it's certainly possible to have a cordial relationship with each other, even if it will never be exactly what you wish it could have been."

He chuckled, and she braced herself for another slightly patronizing comment about her eternal optimism. It didn't come.

Deciding not to press her luck, and hoping she'd at least given him something to think about, she turned her attention to the screen in her lap, reading the first question to him.

The drive passed quickly as they studied. They discussed the material for an hour before taking a break. Ron insisted his brain was full, and he needed time to let the material settle in. Though she laughed, Haley set the netbook aside for a few minutes.

"Tell me everyone's names again. Your sister is Deb, right?"

"Yes. Her sons are Kenny and Bryce."

"And she's a single mom?"

"Divorced," he said with a nod. "Her ex was a real piece of work. Everyone told her that he was a loser before she even married him, but that only seemed to make her more determined to stay with him. He finally ran off with another woman and she hasn't heard a peep from him since. It's been more than a year now."

"That's a shame for her boys."

Ron shrugged. "They're better off without him."

Putting that aside, she asked, "Your brother is Tom?"

"Tommy's the one in jail," he reminded her. "Mick's the one who'll be there today."

"Oh. Sorry."

"No problem. You'll like Mick okay, until he has a couple of beers and gets mad at Dad over something. He gets pretty obnoxious then."

"Maybe they won't quarrel today."

"And maybe these gray skies will clear into a beautiful, sunshiny afternoon, but that's not what I'm expecting."

She glanced at the heavy, dark, oppressive-looking clouds that were already spitting rain against the windshield and shook her head in response to his analogy.

"Is Mick married?"

"Not the last I heard. He's had a string of live-ins, but no one permanent. No kids, as far as I know."

She put that aside for now, too. Other than his parents, who didn't seem particularly happy together from what he'd said, his family history of relationships was hardly encouraging. "What are your parents' names?"

"T.L.—Thomas Lane—and Carolyn Gibson. They'll insist you call them by their first names. Neither one of them likes formality. In Mom's case, she wouldn't want to be reminded that she's that much older. She can't even bear for the kids to call her grandmother. They call her CiCi. Don't ask me why."

She listened to his tone as much as his words when he spoke of his family members, hearing quite a few nuances layered there. Some bitterness. Somewhat dark amusement. But she thought she heard affection buried there, too, even if it was accompanied by old pain.

Or was she simply being an overearnest, aspiring psychiatrist? A common pitfall among medical students, she admitted with a self-chiding grimace.

"I think CiCi is a cute name for a grandmother," she said simply.

He chuckled, but there wasn't a lot of humor in the sound. She noticed that the closer they came to his hometown, the more tension appeared in his face.

She opened the computer again. "Okay. A right hemicolectomy is performed on a fifty-seven-year-old woman with adenocarcinoma who had a preoperative elevation of carcinoembryonic antigen to 144."

Ron nodded to indicate he'd followed her thus far. He seemed much more comfortable discussing colorectal cancer than his family.

They stopped for a stretch break thirty minutes out of Hurleyville, after being on the road more than two hours. Making use of a reasonably clean convenience-store restroom, Haley washed her hands, then fluffed her hair and freshened her lip gloss. She wanted to make a good impression on Ron's family, whatever he said about them.

She had to admit she was a little nervous about meeting them. Partially because of the things Ron had told her. Also because she knew he had called her his girlfriend when he'd told them that he was bringing her. Would that lead to awkward questions neither of them would know how to answer?

Ron waited for her at the car, leaning against the hood to postpone climbing back beneath the wheel. "Ready?"

She nodded and slid into the passenger seat again, reaching for her seat belt.

"Guess there's no need to pull the notes out again. We'd barely have time to get started studying before we arrive."

"Yeah. We'll start again on the way home."

"I hope your family likes the candies I brought."

"They'll love them. You really didn't have to go to all that trouble to make homemade Christmas candies for them."

"Well, your mother told us not to bring anything for the meal. I hated to arrive empty-handed. Besides, I like making Christmas treats. I just wish I'd had time to make and decorate sugar cookies."

"Trust me, the fudge and homemade caramels you brought will be well received. I came by my sweet tooth genetically."

She smoothed her dark brown slacks beneath the seat belt. She'd chosen to wear them with a thin, deep red sweater because the outfit wouldn't wrinkle during the long drive. And maybe because Ron always complimented her when she wore this fitted, scoop-neck sweater, she had to admit privately.

He looked good today, too. She liked the hunter green twill shirt he'd worn with his khaki slacks. It looked good with his sandy hair and bright blue eyes. But then, Ron always looked good to her.

He glanced at her with a smile. "You're looking at me."

"Admiring the view," she quipped, reaching over without thinking to pat his knee.

He caught her hand and lifted it to his mouth, brushing his lips across her knuckles and for just that moment, everything was okay between them again. "Careful, Haley. That was almost a compliment."

She laughed softly, feeling tingles rippling from her hand to her heart. "I'll have to watch that. Wouldn't want your head to get too big."

He squeezed her fingers and released her. Just for fun, she lightly punched his right arm before withdrawing it.

Ron laughed. "Now, that's my Haley."

"His" Haley. Why was it that her breath caught in her throat every time he said that?

The winter-bare rice and soybean fields that made up so much of the northeast Arkansas scenery gave way to the outskirts of Jonesboro, the largest city in the area. Ron pointed out the university where he'd obtained his undergraduate degree as they passed. "Go, Red Wolves."

She laughed and shook her head. "Go, Bears," she insisted, naming her own college team.

"Are there any old friends you'll want to see while you're in town?" she asked, following that line of thought.

He shrugged. "Not really. I still have a couple of friends from high school in the area, and a few college buddies scattered around, but there's no one in particular I want to see today. To be honest, I feel closer to Connor and James these days than anyone from my past. Even Hardik, to an extent. I guess it's that bond forged by getting through those first hellish two years."

"I know what you mean. As much as I still love my old friends, I consider Anne my very closest friend now. And you and James and Connor, of course. I'll always treasure the time we've spent together."

He slanted a frown in her direction. "Not sure how I feel about being just another name on that list."

She flushed a little. "I didn't mean it like that. Of course you're special to me apart from the study group."

"Hmm." He looked ahead again as they left Jonesboro behind and entered the outskirts of a smaller, more rural burg. The road now was an uneven two lane lined with small frame houses and mobile homes and a few newer-looking brick homes.

Downtown Hurleyville showed evidence of a once thriving little community now victim to a changing economy. The old buildings that had once held clothing and fabric and furniture and hardware were now either vacant or filled with second-hand merchandise and dollar store wares. She supposed the locals drove into Jonesboro to the shopping malls and super-stores there for their purchases. Ron pointed out the old train station that had long since been abandoned to nature.

Crumbling old towns like this always made Haley a little sad. She loved nothing more than to visit one of the many rural towns in Arkansas that had reclaimed their heritage and managed to revitalize their old downtowns with new attractions. Perhaps Hurleyville's administration would figure out some similar strategy in the future, she suggested.

Ron shrugged. "We've had the same mayor for almost as long as I can remember. He's content to just watch the town die, apparently, and no one seems to have the time or energy to contest him. My dad actually considered running against him a couple of times, but he's not exactly a pillar of the community, himself."

He braked to allow a couple of farm-equipment trailers to pass, then made a left turn onto a rutted asphalt road. They drove past a pasture full of cattle, another that held a few horses, and then a mobile home on concrete blocks with broken toys scattered across the yard.

Considering the way Ron had spoken of his home, she was rather surprised when he finally pulled into the driveway of a tidy buff-colored brick and off-white siding ranch house styled similarly to her parents' home. The grass and flower beds were brown for winter now, but she saw signs that flowers bloomed around the house in the summer. The concrete driveway looped around the house and she could see a large garage in the back, surrounded by vehicles of all different makes and models.

"It looks like your dad's car repair business is thriving."

"Yeah. He does a good job. Folks around here can't always afford new vehicles, so they depend on Dad to keep their transportation running. He works on farm equipment, too, sometimes. Tractors, mostly."

Climbing out of his car, she studied the surroundings again while he retrieved the basket of candies and a large bag of wrapped Christmas gifts from the backseat. Ron might not have grown up in luxury, but it looked as though the family hadn't exactly lived in abject poverty, either. She imagined they had struggled at times, but then so had her own family. Neither of them had been raised in the financial comfort Anne and James seemed to take rather for granted.

Anne and James weren't obnoxious about their privileged backgrounds, but Haley always sensed that neither quite understood what it was like for their families to have to worry about whether they could pay the light bill from month to month. Her family had been in that position a few times, and Ron's probably had, too, while his dad had established his auto repair business. It was another bond between them, she supposed, despite the other differences in their childhoods.

Ron drew a deep breath as he looked at the unassuming house. And then he turned to Haley with a crooked smile. "It's not too late to change your mind."

Shaking her head in reproach at him, she reached for the candy basket. "Let's go see your family."

Ron didn't bother to ring the bell at the front door, but turned the knob and stepped inside, motioning for Haley to accompany him.

"Hey," he called out in the small entryway. "I'm here."

At first glance, Haley noted that the inside of the house was as neat as the outside. A few inexpensive prints hung on the white painted walls, and three red silk poinsettias in craft-store-decorated pots were arranged on an old-looking sideboard in the foyer.

The smells wafting into the foyer from the back of the house were mouthwatering. Haley could hear children squealing in another room, Ron's nephews, she assumed. All very homey and welcoming.

A short, comfortably padded woman with tousled, collar-length hair the same sandy color as Ron's bustled out to welcome them. "There y'all are. We were wondering what was keeping you."

"We're exactly on time, Mom." Ron leaned over to kiss his mother's cheek. "Something smells great."

"It should. I've been cooking for three days getting everything ready for today." Carolyn turned to Haley with open curiosity. "Hello. Since my son hasn't bothered to introduce us, I'm Carolyn—we don't bother with the Mr. and Mrs. part here. You must be Haley."

She hadn't even given Ron a chance to introduce them, but he didn't bother to protest, merely smiled wryly.

"It's very nice to meet you, Carolyn. Thank you for having me today."

"Haley made Christmas candies for the family, Mom."

Carolyn took the offered basket with a light of anticipation in her blue eyes, though she shook her head with a cluck of her tongue. "Dad and I don't need all this candy on our diets, but it was nice of you to think of us, Haley. Y'all come in."

"They'll eat and enjoy every piece of it," Ron murmured into Haley's ear as they followed his mother into the living room. "That was her idea of expressing gratitude."

She didn't have a chance to respond.

Two men sat in recliners facing the television in the living room, one younger, one older, both holding cans of beer.

Another man sat on the worn couch next to a blonde who had to be Ron's sister, judging from the resemblance. Two little boys—maybe five and three—played on the carpeted floor in one corner of the room beneath a colorfully decorated Christmas tree.

Only one of the men stood when Haley entered, the dark-haired, dark-eyed man from the couch. With his Hispanic coloring and features, it was obvious that he was not Ron's brother.

Carolyn harrumphed loudly. "Don't you guys see we have a guest? Get up and introduce yourself, Mick. You, too, T.L."

Dutifully, the other men lowered the footrests of their recliners and rose to their feet, though Haley noticed the older man looked reluctant to tear his eyes from the football game.

"Everyone, this is Ron's girlfriend, Haley Wright. Don't expect Ron to introduce you to her. Haley, this is my husband, T.L., our son, Mick, our daughter, Debra and her boyfriend, Luis Rodriguz—"

"Ramirez," Deb corrected with a sigh.

Her mother ignored her. "And Deb's sons, Kenny and Bryce, are back there playing with their trucks."

"It's nice to meet everyone," Haley assured them with a smile. "Please sit back down, I don't want to keep you from your game."

Nodding in approval, Ron's father immediately took his seat again.

"I brought some gifts to put under the tree, Mom," Ron said, hefting the bulging bag.

She nodded. "Put them under, then. We'll open gifts after lunch, since Deb won't be coming back for Christmas Day."

The broad hint of accusation in the comment made her daughter sigh again.

Having arranged the gifts beneath the tree, Ron came back around to shake Luis's hand. "Nice to meet you, Luis. I didn't realize Deb was seeing anyone."

"That's why I wanted to come this weekend." Deb flashed her left hand, revealing a sparkle of diamond. "Luis and I are getting married. Sometime next summer, probably. I've already told everyone else."

"Yeah? Welcome to the family, Luis." Ron shook his hand again, then turned to brush a kiss across his sister's cheek. "I hope you'll be very happy together, Deb."

"Now that everyone's finally here, we can go ahead and eat before the food gets cold," Carolyn announced from the doorway. "T.L., turn off that TV and come to the dining room. You're saying the blessing."

"Why don't you say the blessing this time?" T.L. argued, though he climbed to his feet again.

"Don't start with me," his wife told him with a shake of her finger. "This is as close as a family Christmas as we're going to get this year, since Deb's determined to spend the holiday in Florida. Least you can do is say the blessing."

"Looks like we're going to eat now," Ron murmured to Haley, placing a hand at her back to escort her to the dining room.

Giving him a "behave yourself" look, she followed the crowd.

During the noisy, rather chaotic meal, she saw some of the issues Ron had warned her about. Carolyn was a chronic complainer, seemingly incapable of being completely satisfied with anything. Her rather taciturn husband, a thicker, more weathered version of Ron, made a habit of tuning her out except to occasionally complain back at her. Deb, a thinner, more finely honed clone of her mother, had a chip on her shoulder that Haley could almost see, as if daring anyone to offend her—which seemed to happen on a fairly regular basis.

Mick, an odd mixture of both his parents, sported a thinning ponytail and several prominent tattoos. He seemed to be an observer, sitting back and watching everyone else while he ate, his thoughts hard to read. Occasionally he made a wry observation or told an amusing anecdote about his life on the road.

Ron had implied that Mick had a temper. That wouldn't surprise Haley. She suspected he'd have to in the rough-and-tumble life he seemed to favor. She sensed a lot of tension between Mick and his parents. Had he chosen a life on the road to get away from that tension, or was it caused by the path he'd taken? Maybe a little of both.

There was love here, she reflected, eating the excellent, country-style food and watching Ron's family try so hard to interact with each other. But it was masked in habitual bickering and criticism, clouded by the haze of beer and smothered beneath years of hurt. No one mentioned the missing member of the family, but even Haley felt his absence, and she'd never met Tommy.

Most of the initial conversation centered around Deb's engagement, Carolyn's trials in her job as a middle-school secretary and the stories Mick told about his life on the road. Ron participated, as she tried to do when it seemed appropriate, but she noted that there were few questions about his life. Maybe because the others just didn't know what to ask about medical school?

They certainly didn't hold back on their criticism of him. He didn't call enough, didn't visit enough. His dad wanted to know why he'd bought the particular vehicle he was driving.

"Because I needed a new one and I got a good deal on that one from a friend's brother," Ron replied.

"Should have asked me first. I'd have told you that model's nothing but trouble."

"I haven't had any trouble with it so far."

"You will. And don't expect me to keep it running for you. I don't work on those. More trouble than they're worth."

"Don't worry, I won't ask."

The predicted storm hit while they were having dessert. Rain hammered the roof and slammed against the windows while thunder and lightning made the children whimper. Deb comforted her little one. Her mother plied the older one with cake and pie to distract him from the weather. Deb criticized her mother for giving the child too many sweets, to which Carolyn retorted that she knew all about raising children, thank you very much.

T.L. and Mick began to quarrel about some arcane sports statistic, causing Ron to sigh and mutter beneath his breath. "Great. Here we go."

"I'm going to clean up this mess and then we'll open our presents," Carolyn announced, standing to gather the dirty dishes. "You all go into the living room and entertain the babies until I get done in here."

Haley sprang to her feet. "Let me help you."

Carolyn gave her a look that might have held a touch of approval for making the offer, though she shook her head. "I don't like anyone else messing around in my kitchen. No one knows where everything goes, and I end up searching for stuff for days. But thanks for offering, hon."

"She's serious, you know," Deb said with a wry shrug for Haley. "She doesn't let anyone mess around in her kitchen. And then she'll spend the rest of the day complaining about how much work she has to do around here."

Frowning, Carolyn pointed a serving spoon at her daughter. "Watch your mouth."

"I'm thirty years old, Mom. Don't talk to me like I'm still a teenager."

"You treat your mama with respect when you're in this house," her father ordered over his shoulder from the doorway. "Don't matter how old you are."

"Just let it go, Deb," Mick said somewhat wearily when his sister looked prepared to continue the argument. "They're always going to say stuff like that."

Deb rounded on her older brother. "Don't you tell me what to do, either!"

"Deb, why don't you and I show Luis and Haley Mom's prized African violets?" Ron suggested quickly. "Dad and Mick can watch the boys for a minute."

She nodded slowly. "All right. Bryce, honey, go with Uncle Mick. You can play with your trucks again and then we'll open presents when I come back in, okay?"

Still nervous of the booming thunder, Bryce was lulled only by the promise of presents. He allowed himself to be herded into the other room with his brother, uncle and grandfather.

The African violets were displayed on shelves built into a large greenroom off the back of the house. Haley imagined the room would be filled with sunshine on pretty days, bringing a reminder of summer inside even on cold winter days.

"This is a lovely room," she said, touching a fingertip carefully to a velvety purple petal. "The flowers are beautiful."

"My mother's pride and joy," Deb said, turning a lavender plant an inch in its stand to better display the blooms. "She's been raising them since before Ron was born."

Watching the storm sweeping across the yard beyond the greenroom glass, Haley commented, "This room is wonderful. I'm sure she loves sitting out here with her flowers."

She motioned toward a little wicker table and two matching chairs arranged next to the far wall.

"Dad built it for her for their twentieth anniversary, almost twenty years ago," Ron commented. "He spent several months working on it. She's always complained that it should have been larger, and she wishes it had a little more southern exposure and she wishes he'd put in a few more electrical outlets, but she really does enjoy the room, for the most part."

"As much as Mom enjoys anything," Deb agreed with a heavy sigh.

"I'm sure she loves it," Haley repeated.

She suspected Carolyn had obsessive-compulsive tendencies. The very tidy house, the perfectly arranged violets, the fact that no one except her worked in her kitchen—all pointed to control issues she'd have difficulty reining in without treatment. Those same tendencies would make her very trying to live with, especially for people who didn't understand the underlying neuroses.

And there she went falling into psych-think again, she thought with a slight shake of her head.

"You weren't kidding about your mother, were you?" Luis asked Deb, throwing a cautious glance in the direction of the open doorway.

Deb laughed shortly. "No. I wasn't kidding. Why do you think I moved to Florida?"

She patted her fiancé's arm. "I'm so glad now I did make that move."

Luis smiled down at her, and Haley thought they made a nice-looking couple. They seemed very much in love. She hoped this marriage would make Deb happier than her first one had. Haley had watched Luis with the boys during lunch, and he seemed quite fond of them. Perhaps Deb had found what she'd been searching for in him.

She wondered if Mick would ever acquire whatever he was looking for during his restless travels. She was glad Ron had found medicine, which gave him a purpose in his life, a goal to work toward, the validation he hadn't heard much from his family.

There were other reasons she was happy Ron had entered medical school, she admitted to herself. She understood exactly what Deb meant when she'd said she was pleased her path had led her to Luis. Haley couldn't imagine never having known Ron. No matter how much heartache he might cause her in the long run.

Deb shared a faint smile with her brother. "I guess they're getting a taste of what it's going to be like to be a part of this family, huh, Ron? Luis hasn't taken to his heels yet. Maybe Haley won't, either."

"Oh, I—" Haley swallowed her instinctive, almost panicky assertion that Deb was misinterpreting her relationship with Ron. This wasn't the time to get into those details. She settled for a somewhat sickly-looking smile, instead.

"All right, y'all get in here and let's open presents," Carolyn called from inside. "These boys are getting antsy."

"We're coming, Mom, jeez." Rolling her eyes, Deb caught Luis's hand in hers and led him toward the door, still muttering about her mother's impatience.

Haley glanced at Ron when she turned to follow them. He was looking at her with a frown that made her steps fumble just a bit. He did not look particularly happy with her.

"Um—?"

He smoothed his expression immediately. "We'd better hurry before Mom really gets impatient."

While thunder continued to boom outside, he ushered her into the other room before she could say anything else.

"We're under a tornado watch," Ron's dad announced when everyone entered the living room. He nodded toward the television screen, where a colorful map covered the lower part of the screen, the counties under severe weather watches highlighted in red and blue. "Until ten o'clock tonight."

"A watch, not a warning?" Deb confirmed, casting a quick eye at her children.

"Yeah. Just a watch."

Having lived in Arkansas all his life, Ron didn't get too perturbed over a watch situation. The family would leave the

TV on—which they usually did, anyway—and keep an eye on those colored boxes, but it was hardly time to head for the hallway.

A hard gust of wind buffeted the house. Bryce whimpered.

"Let's open presents, Brycie," his grandmother said, taking him into her lap.

"Good thing the leaves are off the trees." Ron's dad nodded toward the windows as he spoke to whomever was listening. "That wind would be knocking some limbs off."

Their mother talked Mick into distributing gifts, because that had been his job for years and she was nothing if not consistent in her nagging. Mick sighed heavily, but didn't bother arguing. He passed out the presents with a notable lack of ceremony, simply lobbing packages in the general direction of the recipients named on the tags. Their mom fussed at him for his carelessness, but she'd have criticized, anyway, so Ron didn't blame him for not paying any attention to her.

Showing a resemblance to her mother she would have furiously denied, Deb shook her head when she looked up from a few of the gifts she and her sons had already opened. "Knitted scarves, Mom? What are we supposed to do with these in Florida?"

Ron frowned and looked quickly at his mother, hoping Deb's careless comment hadn't hurt her feelings. But Carolyn merely shrugged and said gruffly, "I've got to have something to do around here in the evenings and on the weekends while your father's out messing with those cars fourteen hours a day. It's not like I've got anyone to talk to. Besides, I know there's an occasional cool night in Florida. They're always talking on the news about having to save the oranges from the occasional frost."

Shrugging in what might have been an acknowledgment of the point, Deb looked more pleased with the frilly red nightgown she opened next. The kids seemed happy with the toys their grandparents had given them, their handmade scarves dumped carelessly into a corner beneath a pile of torn wrapping paper.

Haley looked surprised when Mick tossed a tidily wrapped box into her lap. She looked at Ron, who sat beside her on the couch. He shook his head. "Not from me."

He wasn't surprised his mother had provided a gift for Haley. Mom would consider it bad manners to open presents in front of Haley and not make sure she had something, too. He was certain Luis had at least one gift, also.

He watched Haley peel away the paper, her eyes alight with anticipation. She loved this sort of thing, he thought indulgently. Family. Traditions. Presents. She didn't even seem overly daunted by his family. Though she had certainly looked stunned when Deb had made a passing comment about Haley joining the family. Apparently, the very idea had been enough to send her figuratively reeling backward.

"Oh, Carolyn, this is beautiful." Both looking and sounding awed, Haley lifted the thick, black knit scarf to her cheek, snuggling against the soft-looking yarn. There was just a touch of sparkle to the scarf, which echoed the glow in her eyes when she looked at his mom. "I love it. Did you really make this yourself?"

Carolyn nodded. "Wasn't sure what colors you like. I figured everyone can use a black scarf."

"It's perfect. It'll go with almost everything I own. Thank you so much."

Carolyn's lips curved, and Ron could tell she was pleased by Haley's sincerity. "You're welcome."

"My grandmother tried to teach me to knit when I was a girl, but I could never quite get the hang of it. I know I'd never be able to knit a pattern this intricate."

Ron was amused to see his mother actually preen a little. "It wasn't an easy pattern," she admitted frankly. "Had to put in some late hours to finish it since Ron didn't give me a lot of notice that he was bringing you. But I wanted you to have something nice to open."

"You didn't have to go to so much trouble. But I'll treasure this." Haley was already looping the scarf around her neck, even though it was warm enough in the room without it.

"Maybe I can give you a few pointers about knitting sometime. It's really not all that difficult. Your grandmother probably just didn't know how to teach it."

"I'd like that," Haley said simply, though Ron doubted she believed that knitting lesson would ever actually happen.

Deb was looking at Haley with a slight frown. Maybe Haley's visible pleasure in the gift made Deb aware of her own less-gracious reaction. "You never taught me to knit, Mom."

"I tried, didn't I?" Carolyn retorted. "You wouldn't sit still long enough to learn. Never would listen when I tried to tell you anything."

Ron made an effort to quickly lighten the mood by tossing his own red scarf around his neck with a flourish. "Thanks, Mom. Now all I need is a bull to fight."

"Bullfighters don't wear scarves, Uncle Ron. They wear capes," Kenny piped up.

"Smart boy," T.L. approved with a nod for his oldest grandson.

"You don't let them watch bullfights, do you, Debra? That's much too violent for children."

Deb sighed gustily. "Of course I don't let them watch bullfights, Mother. Honestly, what a question. He's only seen matadors on cartoons."

"Sounds like you're letting them watch violent cartoons."

"How do you like the earrings I got you, Mom?" Ron asked quickly. "Haley helped me pick them out."

"They're nice," his mother replied. "A little bigger than the ones I usually wear. Guess I can wear them to church. Lord knows I never get to go anywhere else where I can dress up nice."

Haley made a little sound beside him that might have been a hastily swallowed chuckle. He didn't dare look at her, or he'd bust out laughing and they'd both be in the doghouse.

"Oh, wait, I forgot. I brought something for the boys," Mick said, bounding to his feet. "Left them out in my truck. I'll run get them."

The boys bounced excitedly, eager to see what else they'd collected for this early Christmas celebration.

Mick returned quickly, bearing an enormous stuffed animal beneath each arm. A purple gorilla for Bryce, and a big orange dinosaur for Kenny. The toys were almost as big as the boys, themselves—and looked suspiciously like giant carnival prizes.

The boys fell on the toys with hoots of delight, wrestling with their huge new friends on the carpet.

"Mick, what were you thinking?" Deb scolded, holding her hands to her face in distress. "How are we supposed to get those home? They'll take up the whole backseat of the minivan."

"We'll manage, Deb," Luis murmured, his expression rueful as he looked at his future stepsons, who clutched their newest toys possessively in response to their mother's criticism.

"Honestly, Mick, sometimes you just don't use good sense," his mother chided, looking in disapproval at the gifts.

Ron couldn't hold it in any longer. He started to laugh, and a moment later heard Haley giggling beside him. Mick joined in, proving he'd known all along exactly what reaction the outsized toys would receive from Deb and his mother. Luis looked as though he would like to laugh, too, but didn't dare, while Deb and their mom watched them all in exasperation. But Ron thought he saw his mother's lips twitch before she turned away to start gathering the discarded wrapping paper littering her carpet.

Chapter Ten

The boys finally gave in to exhaustion and were tucked reluctantly into bed for naps after the gift exchange. Deb and Luis planned to spend the night and leave for Florida the next morning.

"Don't know why you and Haley don't stay, too, rather than going out in that nasty weather," Carolyn grumbled to Ron as she served coffee to the adults in the living room. She'd set out Haley's candies on a holiday plate on the coffee table, and Ron noted that his dad was helping himself liberally to the fudge, despite the huge meal they'd eaten so recently.

Carolyn noticed, too. She reprimanded her husband for eating too many sweets, then moved the plate a little closer to him so he could reach it better.

"We can't stay, Mom," Ron said. "We both have to be at the hospital very early Monday morning. Before dawn. And we have shelf exams in two weeks, so we need to study as much as we can tomorrow."

"What are shelf exams?" Deb asked, returning to the room after tucking in her sons.

"Medical board exams," Ron explained. "We have them after every rotation to cover everything we were supposed to learn in lectures and practice."

"You have tests all the time, don't you? Seems like every time I talk to you you're studying for a test," Mick commented.

Ron chuckled. "Yeah, pretty much."

"Don't know why you'd want to go through that, as much as you hated studying back in school."

Ron shrugged. "It's what I have to do to get where I want to be."

"He didn't want to do real work," his dad muttered. While he pretended to be joking, there was just enough of a dig in his tone to make Haley move a bit restlessly beside Ron.

"Doesn't like getting his hands dirty," T.L. added, jerking a chin in the general direction of his garage. "He was worthless in the shop."

The others laughed and nodded in agreement. Ron's smile was wry as he thought about just how hard and dirty medical school could get.

Sensing Haley was becoming indignant on his behalf, he rested a hand lightly on her knee. There was no need for her to waste her breath defending him. She would never convince his family he was physician material.

"You're right, Dad. I was a hopeless case when it came to working on cars."

"Weren't any good as a carnie, either," Mick asserted. "Nor at selling cars or doing landscape work."

"Why do you think I went to medical school?" Ron shot back with a lazy grin. "It was pretty much the only thing I hadn't tried yet."

"And people really let you treat their sick children?" Deb glanced toward the back of the house where her boys slept as if unable to conceive of trusting their care to her brother's hands.

"I'm not a doctor yet, Deb. I'm still just learning. I have a lot of supervision now, and several years to go before I'll be fully responsible for treating patients."

"That's good, I guess."

"Didn't Ron save your son's life once, Deb?" Haley seemed unable to resist asking.

Ron winced. The others all looked at him, as if wondering just how much he'd embellished that story in the retelling.

"I don't know if he saved Kenny's life," Deb argued vaguely. "He just pulled a piece of candy out of his mouth."

Ron bit his lower lip as he remembered the panic that had coursed through him when he'd seen Kenny's purpling skin. The child had been limp and still in his arms, his eyes already glazing, and Ron had been painfully aware that there'd been no time to waste getting air into the little lungs. Sticking his finger in Kenny's mouth had been pure instinct, half-remembered training from a high school first aid course. He'd never heard anything more beautiful than the boy's first ragged cough when the candy was dislodged.

"I seem to remember you doing a lot of screaming and hollering," Mick murmured to Deb. "You sure thought the kid was dying at the time."

"Takes more than pulling candy out of a kid's mouth to make a man a doctor," T.L. commented.

"At least you're sticking with this course so far." Carolyn's approval was cloaked in a touch of amazement as she spoke to her youngest child.

She glanced at Haley. "I have to warn you, Ron's never been known as the stick-to-it type. I can't tell you how many clubs he joined and sports he started, only to up and quit when he got bored or when it got too hard. I saved and bought him a clarinet 'cause he wanted to be in the band, only for him to quit after just a few weeks…"

"I asked for a trumpet," Ron mumbled.

"…and then I got him an electric guitar when he was in high school, but he didn't stick with that, either."

She didn't add that she'd forbidden him to play the guitar in the house because it made too much noise.

"Yeah. Hard to see Ron hanging in for another five or six years of schooling," Mick said with a skeptical grin. "What's the next plan, bro? Going to try fighting fires?"

"I just might. Or maybe I'll be a mortician. I've been keeping that as a Plan B in case I wash out of med school. You know, if I can't save 'em, might as well bury 'em."

The others laughed again, but Haley was notably unamused.

"I think you're all underestimating the commitment it has taken for Ron to get as far as he has," she said firmly, unable to keep quiet any longer.

Ron gave a slightly muffled groan, which he knew she heard, but she swept on.

"Ron had to finish college with a grade point average in the top ten percent of his entire class. He had to study for and take the six-hour-long MCAT, and earn a score high enough to get him an interview for medical school—which he did. He had to make a good enough impression on his college professors so that they would write excellent recommendation letters for him—which they did. And then he had to do well in his medical school interviews to be accepted over quite a few who were turned away."

"He was an alternate, wasn't he?" Deb asked with a slight shrug.

Ron saw the rare temper leap into Haley's amber eyes, but she appeared to make an effort to bank it.

"He was still one of the select students chosen to start medical school immediately after earning his bachelor's degree. Since then, he's made it through two and a half grueling, relentless, horribly difficult years of lectures and memorization and exams and evaluations. He did well in his classes, he passed Step 1 of the licensure process on his first attempt, and he has excelled in clinical rotations. He even saved another child from choking at the ballpark a few months ago. I don't know how close your little Kenny was to choking, but that other little boy was already turning blue by the time Ron took over."

"Kenny was turning blue, too, remember, Deb?" Carolyn looked at her youngest son as if seeing him in a slightly different light. He didn't delude himself that Haley was actually changing the way his family viewed him, but he appreciated her words, anyway.

"He was, a little," Deb conceded. "I thanked you at the time for what you did for him, if you'll remember, Ron."

Ron shrugged self-consciously. "He's my nephew, Deb. Of course I was going to do whatever I could to help him."

Grinning behind his scruffy five-o'clock shadow, Mick nodded toward Haley. "This one's got your back, bro. Better hang on to her."

"I'm doing my best," Ron replied as Haley fell quiet beside him again.

He didn't add that hanging on to Haley was probably another challenge that would prove to be too much for him.

A few minutes later, Ron stood and walked to the window, looking out at the sky. The rain had subsided some, and the winds were calmer. A low rumble of thunder sounded occasionally, following distant flashes of lightning, but he thought maybe the storm was easing. There were still tornado watches between here and Little Rock, but most of the really bad weather seemed to be west of them. TV forecasters predicted another round of storms to hit central Arkansas during the night, but Ron thought they had just enough time to get home before it all began again.

"We'd better leave while we've got a break in the weather," he said, glancing toward the moving radar on the television screen. Green bands of rain striped the western half of the state, all moving this way, but there were no active tornado warnings at the moment. They were probably going to hit some downpours on the way home, but his all-wheel-drive car was dependable on wet roads, despite his dad's derision of the model.

His mother protested, of course.

"Let 'em go, Carolyn," her husband ordered. "They don't need to be out too late in this weather."

Conceding the point, she bit back any further arguments.

Mick helped Ron carry his gifts out to the car. They came back in shaking off water droplets and earning another reprimand from their mother.

"Thanks, Mick."

His brother nodded. "I'll see you when I see you, bro. Good luck with your cabinet exam."

"Shelf exam."

"Yeah, whatever."

Ron shook his brother's hand. "Take care of yourself."

He turned to hug his sister. "Kiss the boys for me when they wake up. Sorry I can't stay to visit them longer, but I'd like to get Haley home before those storms fire up again, if I can."

While his brother and sister told Haley how much they'd enjoyed meeting her, and bade her to join them again sometime, Ron shook Luis's hand. "Hope you know what you're getting yourself into, Luis."

The older man smiled. "I've got a pretty good idea. Deb's worth it."

"Take care of her and my nephews."

"I will."

Ron felt the familiar tension in the back of his neck when he turned to his father. He'd spent his entire life trying to please his dad, and always feeling as if he fell short. "See you, Dad. Thanks for the gifts."

"Your mama did all the shopping. But, uh, thanks for the hunting jacket. That's a nice one."

"Mom said she thought you could use another one."

"She shouldn't be telling y'all anything to get for me. Need to save your money for yourselves."

"I'm doing okay, Dad."

His father nodded shortly. "I know you are, son. You keep at that doctoring, you hear? Sounds like you're doing pretty good with it."

So maybe Dad had listened to Haley, after all. At least for now. "Yeah, I'll stick with it. I'll talk to you later, okay?"

"Yeah. Get a move on now, and call your mama when you get home safe. She'll be worried."

"I will."

His mother walked them to the door. She looked out with a worried eye. "I don't like the looks of those clouds. I wish you'd just stay the night."

"We'll be okay, Mom." He leaned over to kiss her lined cheek. "You outdid yourself today. I know it was a lot of trouble, but everything was perfect."

"It was a lot of trouble," she agreed, then smiled faintly. "But it was worth it. Felt good to have my kids home."

He saw the sadness darken her eyes, and he knew what she was thinking. "Tommy will be out soon, Mom. Maybe he'll turn his life around for the better this time."

She sighed heavily, glancing quickly at Haley, her embarrassment plain. His mother took her oldest son's failings very personally, and refused to accept that Tommy's demons—and his choices—were his own. "Your dad and I are going to see him next weekend. Want me to tell him anything from you?"

"Tell him I said hello." He almost added a Merry Christmas for his brother, but decided that sentiment might not be quite appropriate.

Haley thanked his mother prettily for welcoming her to the family holiday celebration, expressing her gratitude one more time for the hand-knit scarf.

"We hope to see you here again soon," Ron's mother replied, and he could tell she was sincere in the invitation. She slanted a look his way. "Assuming you two don't think you're too good for the likes of us once you're fancy doctors and all."

Ron frowned. "Don't even think that, Mom. Whatever issues we might have among us, this is still my family. Nothing's ever going to change that. Maybe someday we'll even figure out how to just love each other without the other stuff."

She patted his arm. "I do love you, Ronnie."

"I love you, too, Mom. I'll call you Christmas, if not before, okay?"

Blinking rapidly, she nodded and motioned toward the door. "Get on now. You drive carefully, you hear? If it starts storming, pull over."

"We will. 'Bye, Mom."

She closed the door behind them when they ran out into the gray drizzle.

The windshield wipers beat a steady rhythm against the glass as Ron drove south, away from his family home. It was just after 4:00 p.m., and darkness was already falling, partly because of the short days of early winter, partly because of the thick cloud cover.

Haley didn't immediately reach for her netbook as they got underway. She just wasn't up to studying right then. Judging from the slight weariness in the set of Ron's shoulders, he wasn't, either.

"Well?" he said without looking at her, when he'd been driving for almost twenty minutes in silence. "Were they what you expected?"

She turned her head against the back of the seat to study him in the gloomy gray light. "I've seen much worse families."

"So have I, for that matter, but they're still difficult. I will say that everyone was on their best behavior pretty much today. Maybe because you and Luis were there. Dad only had a couple of beers, he and Mick only got into two or three arguments, Deb didn't burst into tears once and Mom didn't complain nearly as much as usual."

Haley found it hard to imagine the woman complaining any more, but she supposed Ron knew best. "Maybe they're just trying harder to get along. And maybe Deb was in a better mood because she's happier. She looked crazy about Luis."

Ron nodded. "Seems like a decent guy. Mom made a few comments behind his back about his Hispanic heritage, but she's not really a bigot. She's an equal opportunity criticizer."

Haley wondered what Carolyn might be saying about *her,* but she wasn't going to worry about it. "Sorry I lectured them when they were making fun of you. I tried to keep quiet, but they were starting to annoy me, ganging up on you that way."

"It's okay. I appreciated you taking up for me. But I'm used to it."

"They were out of line."

He shrugged. "They had some justification for the things they said. I did start and stop a lot of things in the past. Even college, the first time. You can't really blame them for expecting me to quit this, too."

"After four years of college and two and a half years of med school? I'd say you've proven you're sticking with it this time."

He shrugged. "That's the plan. Unless something goes wrong, of course."

She sighed. "You want to hear some armchair psycho-analysis?"

He chuckled in response to her wording, though he kept his eyes focused on the wet road ahead. "Sure. Go ahead."

"I think one reason you kept quitting things is because you never thought you could do them well enough. Your parents are so critical that you could be forgiven for thinking you could never please them. It wouldn't take much to expand that mind-set to thinking you might as well not invest too much of yourself if you couldn't win, anyway."

"Hmm."

She couldn't tell if he agreed, disagreed, or was just humoring her. "Well?"

"Well, what?"

"Could my theory be at least somewhat credible?"

"There's some truth in it."

"Your mother probably has OCD, you know."

"My mother definitely has OCD. I've known that for years."

"Oh." Only a little deflated, she said, "You didn't mention it."

"I told you she's impossible to please."

"Well, yes, but not that it's partially because she can't really help herself."

"Took me a few years to figure that out."

A hard gust of wind buffeted the car. She saw Ron's hands tighten on the wheel.

"Why don't you turn on the radio?" he suggested. "We really should be listening to the weather reports."

Rain swept in curtains across the road ahead as she reached for the knob. "It seems to be getting worse again, doesn't it?"

"Picking up some."

A somber male voice read weather updates on the airways. Haley frowned a little. It sounded as though the system was moving quickly in from the west. The western half of the state was under a new tornado watch. "Hope we get home before that gets to Little Rock."

"Me, too. If we have to, we'll pull over somewhere. Have a leisurely dinner while we wait for it to blow over."

She nodded. "Not that I'm hungry yet. Your mom made so much food."

"She'll complain for days about how tired she is from all that work. But she seemed to enjoy having us there."

"I think she did."

"She liked you, Haley. I could tell."

"That's nice. I hope you don't think I dislike your family. I don't, you know."

He slanted her a quick smile. "I know. You don't really dislike anyone, do you?"

"Well, not many people," she admitted, thinking of a few. "But everyone was very nice to me today."

He took his right hand from the wheel long enough to squeeze her knee. "You're easy to be nice to."

Unexpectedly, she felt her cheeks flood with warmth. How far gone was she that a simple squeeze and an offhanded compliment could make her hands suddenly tremble?

Careful, Haley.

He placed his hand on the wheel again, fighting the gusts of wind. He drove doggedly on, and she didn't want to distract him with conversation. She didn't even try to study during this ride; Ron needed to keep his attention on the wet road. Darkness was falling quickly, though it was hard to distinguish from the already-cloud-darkened skies. Rain fell steadily on the roof and washed across the windows. The radio kept them informed about watches and warnings, informing them that the worst of the storm was still headed their way. Fortunately, there wasn't a lot of traffic on the roads and most of the other drivers were also using caution, though there were the occasional idiots who drove as recklessly as if the weather was completely clear and dry.

The silence had extended for quite some time before Ron spoke again, his voice somber, raised a little above the noise from outside. "What you said to my family? About me being more capable of commitment than they give me credit for?"

Drawn from her own thoughts, she nodded. "Of course you're capable of commitment. There's no way anyone would survive the first two years of med school without being completely dedicated to it."

"I would have thought you'd have agreed with them. As often as we've argued about that very sort of thing, I mean."

She sighed. "The reason we argued in the past was because I hated hearing you sell yourself short. All that talk of quitting and falling back on Plan B, all those doubts about whether you belonged in medical school or whether you would be able to see it through—well, hearing those things just annoyed me because I knew it was all foolishness."

"So you do think I'm capable of making a total commitment, despite what you said to Lydia and Kristie at the party."

Rain hammered harder against the top of the car, sounding even louder than before in the awkward pause that followed his comment. The wipers weren't having much effect against the downpour. She cleared her throat, staring hard out the windshield rather than at him. "Of course you're capable, Ron. You just don't always choose to do so."

She craned her neck to look ahead for a safe place to stop for a while. They were pretty much surrounded by farm and pastureland. There weren't a lot of cars on the road with them; maybe other people had the sense to stay inside during weather like this. But it really hadn't been this bad when they'd left his parents' house, she reminded herself.

"I am going to finish medical school, Haley," Ron said.

"Of course you will. Can you see the road?"

"Yeah, I can see pretty well. You don't have to worry, you know."

She wrinkled her nose. "I'm trying not to worry. But this weather is really getting ugly. I don't know whether it would be better to keep moving toward home or pull over somewhere and hope we get another break in the rain."

"I'm still hoping we can get home before that next front line moves into the central part of the state. I'll pull over if I think it's getting too risky to keep driving, but right now it's just a heavy rain. I can drive in that as long as I watch my speed—and the morons don't run us off the road."

He spoke just as a big truck with oversize tires sped past them, throwing up fountains of water from the road, blowing the smaller car slightly sideways on the wet pavement.

"Jerk," Haley muttered.

"That's one word for him," Ron agreed grimly, peering through the semicircular swaths carved by the wipers.

Once he'd steadied the car again, he glanced at her. "I wasn't actually talking about the weather."

She drew her attention from the dark skies ahead. Between the rain on the roof and the droning of the weather reporter on the radio, she was having a little trouble hearing him clearly. "Hmm?"

"When I said you don't have to be nervous, I meant you don't have to worry that I'll hold you back in your career. I know how exclusive those triple-board programs are, but I have no doubt you'll get into one if you want."

Forgetting the weather for the moment, she turned in her seat to stare at him. "What are you talking about?"

He sighed loudly, looking both frustrated and self-conscious. "It's just—well, I know several people lately have warned you that it's hard sometimes for a couple to find residencies in the same hospitals. I know a few have hinted that I could be a liability to you. And then Deb made that comment today that left you looking so nervous, so I thought maybe you should know…never mind. Forget I said anything. Stupid time to bring this up."

She bit her lip. Was he really trying to convince her that he wouldn't interfere in her career plans? Or was he implying he wasn't expecting them to still be together when the time came for applying to residency programs?

A flicker of anger sparked beneath the dull pain his clumsy assurances had left in her chest, and she spoke without bothering to guard her words. "Let me make something clear to you. If I wanted to find a residency program at a hospital that was also a good match for you, I wouldn't care what anyone else said about it. Not our classmates, not our families, not our friends…no one. I make my own decisions. Nor do I think that being with you would ever hold me back in my career, for that matter. I've told you before that I believe you can get into any residency program you want. I was being completely honest."

His jaw tightened as he stared grimly ahead. "I would never want you staying with me because you don't believe in giving up. Sometimes it really is best to walk away. For your own sake."

Her temper flared higher. "And I wouldn't want to stay with someone who wasn't willing to fight against all the odds to keep us together. What's the point of making commitments at all if a person is willing to just walk away when the going gets hard? How can you pour everything you have into anything if you aren't willing to invest whatever it takes to succeed?"

He risked glanced at her again. "Are we talking about school again—or about us?"

"We're talking about whatever is important to you," she answered evenly.

She might as well face it. She had told herself she wouldn't fall in love with him. She had promised herself she could keep it light. That she wouldn't expect too much and therefore wouldn't be disappointed when it inevitably ended. After all, she'd been able to accomplish that goal with other men from her past.

It wasn't the same with Ron.

When had she fallen in love with him? Since they'd become lovers? Sometime during the two years prior to that? The first day she'd met him?

"Haley—"

He cursed when rain lashed the car so hard it nearly blew them sideways. "We're going to have to pull over for a while until this band blows over."

Nodding stiffly, she peered through the torrents. "Looks like a little café up ahead. We could wait in there."

She wasn't hungry, but there was no need to risk both their lives in this weather.

He pulled into the parking lot and as close to the door as he could get. There were only a few other cars in the lot at just before six on this Saturday evening. Either it was too early for the dinner crowd or other people had the good sense to stay out of this storm.

"You want to make a run for it or just sit out here in the car?"

She looked at the sheets of rain between them and the door, weighed the discomfort against a continuation of this painful discussion with Ron. She really didn't think she was ready to hear him confirm that she had offered her heart to a man who wasn't interested in the responsibility of caring for it long-term. Maybe she just wanted to hold on to the fantasy for a little longer.

"Let's go in."

They didn't bother with umbrellas, but simply jumped out of the car and made a dash for it. They shed their wet coats inside the café, hanging them to dry on a coat rack just inside the door. Their pants and shoes were wet, and their hair hung damp and limp, but at least they weren't soaked to the skin.

A waitress with flame-red hair and too much black eyeliner approached them with a commiserative smile. "Pretty bad out there, isn't it? We've got the TV on in the corner over there so we can watch the radar. You know we're under a tornado watch, don't you?"

"Yes, we know." Ron glanced at the screen where a graphic showed almost the entire state covered in boxes depicting thunderstorm warnings, tornado watches and flash-flood warnings. Two serious-looking men in white shirts and loosened ties sat at a news desk, discussing the radar activity they were showing on-screen. "We thought we'd have a bite to eat and wait for the rain to let up a little before we keep driving to Little Rock."

Nodding, she waved a hand tipped with blue nail enamel toward the small dining room. "Just sit wherever you want. I'll bring you a menu. And some coffee?"

"Please," Ron and Haley said in unison.

"Be right with you."

At a quick glance, Haley noted that only a few other people were in the café, counting the two waitresses and whoever was working the kitchen. A family of four sat at a table next to the front glass wall. Mother and father in their late thirties, a boy and girl of maybe nine and twelve, respectively, all talking at once as they ate. An elderly couple—mid-seventies, perhaps?—were silently putting away bowls of soup and a basket of corn bread muffins at a table in the corner. And a younger couple dined on hamburgers and fries while stopping often to coo at the baby sitting in a carrier on a third chair at their table. Occasionally they glanced at the TV and out the windows, keeping an eye on the weather, probably judging when it would be safe to make a run for their car.

Haley doubted that the little establishment often had a full dining room, but she suspected there were usually more here than this. The place was clean and the food looked good. The weather had to be a factor in the lack of business tonight.

"Here's your coffee." The waitress, identified by a name tag as Candi, set steaming mugs in front of them. "Bet you're both chilled with that damp hair."

"We are," Ron answered her with a smile that made her eyelashes flutter. "Thank you, Candi."

She grinned back at him, as people always did. "What can I get y'all to eat?"

"What do you recommend?" Ron asked.

"The burgers are always good. The soup of the day is homemade vegetable beef, and that's pretty good, too. But my favorite is the chicken-fried steak with mashed potatoes and fried okra."

Ron sighed regretfully. "That sounds really good, but we had a big lunch. Guess I'd better just have the soup."

"I'll have the same, thank you," Haley decided. Warm soup sounded good on a day like this, and a light enough dinner after their hearty lunch. Maybe by the time they'd finished eating, the rain would have let up enough to allow them to get underway again.

Candi had their soup on the table in less than five minutes. "This feels more like spring weather than December, doesn't it?"

"It does, indeed." Ron reached for a corn muffin from the heaped basket she'd set in the center of the table.

They were all used to regular tornado watches in the tur-bulent Arkansas springs. It wasn't that they didn't take the reports seriously, but they knew most watches expired without producing the destructive twisters that hit this part of the country so frequently. So they would eat their meals and listen to the talking heads on the screen and when the skies cleared enough, they would be on their way.

A hard blast of wind crashed against the windows and rattled dishes, eliciting a few startled squeaks followed by sheepish, somewhat nervous smiles. The mother of the baby was beginning to look a bit frightened now as she studied the television screen. Haley didn't blame her. The storm was definitely intensifying.

Candi cleared her throat, her eyes a bit anxious, but her smile determinedly professional. "Y'all be sure and save some room for dessert, you hear? Millie makes the best chocolate pie you ever tasted."

Despite his big lunch, Ron perked up at that. "Chocolate pie?"

She laughed. "You'll like it."

Haley frowned and lifted her hands to the sides of her head. "My ears just popped."

Twisting her jaw, Candi nodded. "Mine did, too."

Ron was half out of his seat before the sudden wailing of tornado warning alarms sounded from somewhere outside. "Everyone get away from the windows! Under the tables, quick."

Haley glanced instinctively toward the windows as Ron dashed over to help the older couple out of their seats. Even in the darkness outside, she could see debris rushing sideways past the rain-streaked glass.

"Candi, get down!" She grabbed the waitress's arm and jerked, sending them both tumbling to the floor, half under the bolted-down table.

Chaos descended around them at that instant. She caught just a glimpse of the couple huddled over their baby beneath their own table, and then the lights went out to the sound of breaking glass and hammering impacts against the outside of the building.

Chapter Eleven

Haley's shirt was soaked as she huddled beneath the table with her arms crossed protectively over her head. Something large hit the floor right next to her. She thought she heard screams, but it could have been the shrieking of the wind. The pressure was suddenly so strong that she felt almost as though she were being pulled off the floor. She grabbed the metal base of the table, clinging to it frantically.

The noise abated almost as suddenly as it had intensified. It might have only been seconds, brief minutes at the most, but it felt so much longer.

She was so cold, and so wet. At least part of the roof must have been ripped off above her.

Someone was screaming in earnest now. She took a moment to make sure it wasn't her before lifting her head and opening her eyes.

It was hard to see through the darkness. She heard excited voices crying out, babbling questions and calling for help.

Realizing she had instinctively grabbed her purse when she ducked beneath the table, she shoved a hand into it, pulling out the small, high-beam flashlight she always carried.

Candi still sat beside her, huddled beneath the other side of the table.

"Candi, are you all right?"

Her face white in the beam of the flashlight, the waitress nodded tentatively. "I think so. Damn, that rain is cold."

"Be careful of broken glass when you stand up."

Haley rose carefully, sweeping her flashlight over what had been a tidy dining room. Tables and chairs were scattered among broken crockery now, and shattered light fixtures dangled from the partially missing roof above. At least with the power out they didn't have to worry about electrocution, though there was still the danger of falling debris.

She saw the couple with the baby standing nearby and she stumbled toward them, almost tripping over what must have been a pile of ceiling tiles and insulation. "Are you all right? The baby?"

She could hear the child crying, as was his mother, who had taken him from the carrier and now held him tightly. The father hovered near them, trying to shield them from the rain by holding his coat over them. "I think we're okay," he said. "I got hit in the back of the head by something. Got a goose egg there, but I think I'm okay. We were both covering the baby, so he wasn't hit by anything."

Candi was calling for outside help; Haley could hear the waitress shouting into a cell phone behind her.

"Haley? *Haley!*"

Her knees almost buckled in relief at the sound of Ron's voice. The last she'd seen of him, he'd been rushing toward the wall of windows. Turning her light in that direction, she saw that the entire front of the café had been destroyed. "Ron?"

A hand grabbed her arm, and she was pulled tightly into his arms for a moment. She felt a hard tremor run through him as she clung to him in return. "You're okay?"

She nodded against his chest. "I'm okay. Are you?"

"Going to have some bruises, but I'm all right. We have people hurt over here. Can you help me?"

She straightened away from him. "Of course."

The beam of another powerful flashlight joined Haley's in piercing the wet rain pouring in through the broken ceiling. "Is everyone okay?" a man's voice called from the area of the kitchen.

"Do you have a first aid kit?" Ron called in that direction.

"I'll be right there."

"Ambulances are on the way," Candi announced, already pressing buttons again on the lighted pad of her cell phone. The blue light from the phone threw her face into an eerie silhouette, and her eyes glittered with reaction and excitement.

Haley thought she heard the faint keening of sirens from somewhere in the distance but had no way of knowing if they were ambulances, police or fire trucks, or even if they were headed this way. She didn't know how much damage the surrounding area had sustained, how many people might be hurt and waiting for help.

She and Ron threw themselves into assessing injuries. Identifying themselves as medical students, not doctors, they did what they could to help those who had been hurt. The elderly woman had been cut by a flying piece of glass. In the beam of the flashlight, the cut on her arm didn't look too deep, but they instructed her to lie still and keep the arm elevated in her husband's lap as he sat beside her, staunching the flow with his handkerchief.

The man's breathing was rather labored and his heart rate felt somewhat thready when Haley pressed her fingertips to his neck. "Do you have a heart condition, sir?"

He nodded. "I got nitro tablets in my pocket."

"Do you need to take one? Are you having chest pains?"

He shook his head. "I'm okay. I'll just sit here with Nita and wait for the ambulance."

Hoping he was right, she moved to help Ron with the remaining family.

The boy had been thrown backward by the winds and had fallen on his arm. "It's broken," Ron informed Haley when she knelt beside him to hold the light as he swept his fingers gently over the awkwardly twisted limb.

The boy was trying so hard not to cry, though his breath was catching in swallowed sobs. "It hurts pretty bad."

"I know it does, buddy." Ron rested a hand on the boy's head. "You're doing great. It's okay to cry a little if you need to, okay? I'd probably be crying, too, if I'd broken my arm."

The boy snuffled. "You would?"

"Heck, yes. I'm a real baby. Ask my friend, here, she'll tell you. But you're going to have a cool cast to show off to your friends. You can tell them how brave you've been. Now lie very still while I check on your mom, okay?"

The boy's father had unearthed an umbrella from somewhere. He knelt over his son to shelter him from the rain, though his concern was obviously divided between his son and his wife, who half lay against the bottom of the booth with her daughter hovering tearfully nearby holding another umbrella.

"Will you check on her, doctor?" the dad asked Ron.

"I'm just a medical student, but yes, I'll see what I can do."

Holding the flashlight, Haley moved with Ron to the woman's side. This woman had also been hit by debris, and her face was streaked with blood and rain. She was awake and coherent, having insisted they look after her son first, but Haley suspected the woman would need stitches to close the gaping cut above her left eye.

A large man materialized beside them, holding his flashlight in one hand and a first aid kit in the other. "I'm Mike, the owner of what's left of this place. You needed this?"

"Thanks." Ron dug in the box and found a gauze pad and some tape, which he used to cover the wound temporarily.

"You're doctors?" Mike asked.

"Medical students," Haley replied. "I'm going to check on that other couple again, Ron. I'm a little concerned about the man's breathing. And the young man with the baby got a hard bump on the head. I'll do a quick concussion check, though I think he's okay."

Ron squeezed her hand. "Okay. Call if you need me. I'll check on the boy again."

She straightened. Either the rain was lessening or she was getting used to it; she hardly noticed it now. The sirens outside were definitely getting closer, sounding as though they would arrive very soon. She could imagine that resources were limited in this rural area; she would guess that local emergency services were spread thin until help arrived from surrounding counties.

Candi stood by what had once been the entryway but was now a gaping hole surrounded by twisted metal. "I think I see flashing lights," she called out. "They're getting closer."

Haley stepped toward her. "You'd better move away from that wall," she said with a frown, noting the tangled wiring and dangling construction materials hanging around where Candi stood. Electrocution might not be a danger, but this structure was far from safe. Haley wouldn't breathe easily until everyone was safely out. "Maybe you should come wait over here with me and—"

A wind-driven gust of cold rain hit her directly across the face, cutting off her words. Something creaked loudly in the wind; something else banged.

"Haley, watch—"

She never heard the rest of Ron's warning. One moment she was standing there looking at Candi; the next she was lying on the floor buried beneath what had been the front roof of the diner.

Something covered her face, and something else lay heavily on her chest, making it hard to breathe. There was pain, sharp and angry, but she wasn't sure of its source. It seemed to be coming from several places. She couldn't move, but she didn't know if that was because of the weight on top of her or something else.

She closed her eyes. Maybe she'd just go to sleep for a while. Maybe the pain would be gone when she woke. Ron would take care of her. Ron...

"Haley. Damn it, Haley, open your eyes!"

Ron sounded annoyed with her. She opened her eyes reluctantly, wincing when the beam of a flashlight pierced her pupils.

"Move the light, it's right in her eyes. Haley, honey, open your eyes again. Look at me."

Someone had moved the stuff out of her face and off her chest so that it was easier to breath, but now something seemed to be clogging her brain. She was having trouble thinking clearly. "Ron?"

Her voice sounded slurred, drowsy. Who was screaming now?

Oh, yes. Sirens.

"No, Haley, don't drift off again. Stay with me, okay?"

Pain clawed at the lower half of her body. She tried to squirm away from it, but hands held her still. Someone else was kneeling over her. Candi? What was the owner's name? Mike. She focused on those trivialities to keep from dwelling on the pain. The mounting fear.

She lifted her head, looked downward to where the flashlight beam was focused now. Then wished she'd kept her eyes closed.

Her head fell backward against the hard, wet floor.

"Shouldn't you take that out of her leg?" Candi asked fearfully from somewhere behind Haley's head.

"No!" Ron spoke somewhat more quietly the second time. "No. Don't touch her. The ambulance is almost here."

He held Haley's hand in his. She thought he was gripping tightly, though she could hardly feel his fingers around hers.

"Look at me, Haley. Look at my face."

She blinked hazily up at him. "Just need...to sleep."

"No. I don't want you to go to sleep. I want you to talk to me until the paramedics get here, okay? I don't want you to go to sleep, Haley."

She sighed, feeling the energy draining slowly out of her. "Just going to..."

"Haley, damn it, stay awake! You've never given up on anything in your life, and you're not starting now, do you hear me?" He was almost in her face now, speaking furiously.

Should he really be shouting at her when she was hurt? she thought with an aggrieved scowl.

"I'm not giving up on you, either, Haley. I am never giving up on you, do you hear me? You're stuck with me, got that?"

"Stop yelling at me, Ron." It was so hard to form the words, but she tried to speak with dignity.

"You want me to stop yelling? Stay with me, then."

"When I...wake up, I'm going to...punch your arm so hard."

He raised her hand to his lips. "Okay. You do that. Just don't give up, you hear?"

"Never giving up on you," she whispered, her eyelids lowering despite her effort to hold them open.

He brushed his free hand gently across her face. "I wouldn't let you if you tried."

She thought he said something else, but she didn't hear the words. Only the comforting murmur of his voice as she slipped into the wet darkness.

Two days after the storm, Haley lay in a hospital bed, one leg encased in a bulky brace, other bandages scattered randomly over her body. Her mother and her aunt sat in the two visitors' chairs while her dad and her uncle leaned against the broad windowsill. They'd been there almost since she'd emerged from the operating room after being airlifted to the hospital. As much as she appreciated their loving support, she wished they would leave for a little while.

"Why don't you all go have some dinner?" she suggested. "I'll be fine."

Her mom looked immediately prepared to protest. She hadn't wanted to let Haley out of her sight for the past two days. Even if Haley hadn't been told the full extent of her injuries, her mother's behavior would have let her know just how critical her condition had been by the time she'd arrived in the O.R.

"Really, Mom, I'm fine," she said gently. "Take a break."

The room was filled with flowers and balloons from Haley's friends and classmates. Many of them had been by to check on her, as had several of her instructors.

She'd made Ron and Anne go to their rotations, though both of them had wanted to stay close to her. Ron, especially, had been reluctant to start his new assignment while she lay in this bed. She'd told him there was no need for them both to fall behind in their training.

That thought made a pang go through her. She bit her lip, refusing to give in to her sadness in front of her already-worried parents.

Her mother still looked inclined to refuse to leave her alone, but then the door opened and Ron ambled in. He still wore scrubs from his day on the vascular surgery rotation beneath his crumpled white coat. His hair was tousled, and his pockets were stuffed haphazardly with his tools and materials. His left wrist was wrapped in an elastic bandage, there were two stitches in his chin, and a multicolored bruise darkened his left cheek, all souvenirs of the storm. He'd paid no attention to his own injuries until he'd made sure that she and all the others in the diner were tended to.

Their eyes met and he gave her a smile that almost singed the bed sheet that covered her.

"Maybe we will have some dinner now," her mother said, standing and motioning for the others to accompany her to the door. "We'll see you later, sweetheart."

She brushed a kiss across Haley's cheek before ushering the others out of the room, giving Ron a smile over her shoulder on the way out.

Alone in the room with her, Ron leaned over the bed railing to give her a kiss. "How are you feeling?"

Ignoring the various aches and pains that would plague her for a while yet, she said, "Okay."

"What's wrong?"

"Nothing."

He leaned closer, his eyes locked with hers. "Haley? What's the matter?"

"It's stupid."

He brushed a strand of hair from her face. "What's stupid, honey?"

"I should be so grateful to even be alive. I mean, I could have bled to death from that piece of glass piercing my artery. If anyone had tried to remove it, I probably would have."

"You were lucky." He still got a sick look in his eyes when they talked about her injuries, and she knew he'd been fully aware of how precarious her situation had been. Had medical assistance not been already at the scene, and had a medevac helicopter not arrived very quickly thereafter, the outcome could have been very different. As it was, she'd been rushed into surgery in the nick of time.

She would recover fully. With time to heal and some physical therapy, she'd soon be back in prime condition. She should be very grateful—and she was. But still…

"You're still fretting about missing the next rotation, aren't you?"

She sighed wistfully. "I just hate falling behind."

"Six weeks," he reminded her firmly. "Just the ob-gyn block, that's all you'll miss, and you can make that up next year. The administration has already said they'll work with you to make sure you graduate with the class."

"I know, and I'm grateful to them."

"But you can't stand knowing that the rest of us are going to be going through rotations while you're taking time to recuperate from your injuries, can you?"

He'd described it perfectly. "I just hate being left behind," she muttered, looking away.

"You aren't being left behind. You aren't even the only one who'll miss a rotation and have to make it up during fourth year. It's not that uncommon, you know."

"I know."

"But you still hate it."

"I still hate it."

"You're not giving up, are you? Because you know, you have to keep a positive attitude. You have to put your mind to getting back on your feet. You have to work hard and refuse to surrender even when the going gets tough and things look— Ouch."

She might be flat on her back in a hospital bed, but she could still deliver a pretty satisfying punch to his arm, she thought in satisfaction. "You can stop mocking me now."

"I'm not mocking you," he said, rubbing his forearm. "I'm just showing off all you've taught me during the past two and a half years."

She smiled faintly. "I'm glad something got through."

His smile faded. Pulling one of the chairs close to the bed, he sat beside her, holding her hand. "This is the first chance we've had to be alone since the storm."

"Yes."

"I seem to remember we were in the middle of a discussion before all hell broke loose."

She swallowed hard. Was he really going to continue that talk now? The one that had seemed to be leading to them saying goodbye?

Maybe he was leaving her behind in more ways than one as he moved into his next rotation without her, she thought bleakly.

He searched her face. "Wow. You really are giving up, aren't you?"

"I—" She swallowed hard. "Aren't *you?*"

His fingers tightened around hers. "No. Not this time."

Leaning closer, he held her gaze with his while he spoke in a rush. "All this time, I've been afraid of holding you back. I mean, you're so darned good at all of this. So confident and natural. I honestly believe you can do absolutely anything you set your mind to. Anything."

She was both flattered and dismayed by his words. While she appreciated the compliments, she didn't want to be put on a pedestal by him. That was as unrealistic and distancing as quarreling. "Ron, I'm not—"

"But then I got to thinking," he said, speaking over her as if she hadn't said a word. "I've got a few things to bring to this relationship, too. I keep you grounded—a lot better than a handful of black rocks can do. I make you laugh. I make you mad sometimes, which keeps you from being too much of the sweetness-and-light type, you know? Let's face it, Haley, that can get kind of boring without a little temper to spice it up."

She blinked, trying to figure where he was going with this.

"So we've got a lot of challenges ahead," he continued. Studying his face, she realized he wasn't quite as blasé about his words as he sounded when he forged on. "We have to get you healed again. We have to finish our rotations. We have to ace the rest of our shelf exams. We have to start researching residency programs, and narrowing down places that have something to offer both of us. And then we have to put our minds to charming the residency committees at those places into thinking they absolutely have to have us on their teams."

She bit her lip as she listened to him making such sweeping plans for the long-term future.

But it turned out he was looking even farther ahead. "Once we get into our programs, we'll have two very busy internships to deal with. Won't be easy getting our schedules coordinated. It's going to take a lot of compromising and accommodating."

"You're—" She had to stop to clear her throat. "You're making a lot of assumptions here."

Again, the hint of nerves in his eyes, hidden behind a cocky smile. "Well, yeah, but I'm taking your advice again. I'm being confident. Thinking positive. Refusing to accept the possibility of failure."

"And you're suddenly so positive because...?" she whispered.

"Because I love you so much I can't even conceive of the possibility of giving up this time," he answered simply.

Her heart stopped, then restarted with a hard bump. "Ron—"

"I'll be whatever you need me to be, Haley. Your friend. Your lover. Your own cheerleader. Your safe place to turn in a storm. Whatever you want—I'm here for the duration. If you'll have me."

Blinking rapidly, she forbade herself to cry. "I love you, too, Ron. I have for so long. But I thought you weren't into long-term commitments."

"I've been committed to you since the day I met you," he answered in a tone that was a little hoarse now. "I just needed you to help me find the courage to admit it."

"I seemed to have lacked that courage, myself," she conceded, clinging to his hand. "I've never been so afraid to take a risk before. Maybe because the stakes had just never been this high for me. I pegged you as a heartbreaker from the beginning, Ron Gibson."

He kissed her hand. "My heart is all yours, Haley Wright. I love you with everything I have to give. And I will never walk away from you."

"I'm going to make sure you never want to," she promised him, drawing him toward her for a long kiss of celebration.

Someone tapped on the door, breaking up the embrace. Anne and Liam walked into the room, Anne bearing more flowers, Liam a box of chocolates.

"Are we interrupting anything?" Anne asked, studying their faces with a knowing smile.

Ron grinned, glancing at Haley's radiant, obviously well-kissed face with a surge of masculine pride. "We've just been getting a few things straight between us."

Anne and Liam exchanged a laughing look.

"Hospital rooms seem to be a good place for that," Liam said with a wry smile. "It wasn't that long ago that I was the one lying in a hospital bed while Anne and I got a few things straight."

"As much of our lives are going to be spent in hospitals from now on, I guess it's not so surprising that we'd hold some of our most important conversations there," Anne said with a chuckle. "Um, anything you want to share?"

"Ron and I are going to be staying together," Haley informed them happily. "We're going to graduate together, and look for residencies in the same place."

"And then spend the rest of our lives being happily married doctors," Ron added. "Haley in psychiatry, me in pediatric hem-onc, if all works out well. Which it will," he added hastily, remembering his newfound positivity.

"You're engaged?" Anne asked with a squeal of delight.

Realizing they hadn't actually gotten to that part, Ron gave Haley a quick, questioning look.

"Yes," she said, addressing the reply to both Anne and him. "We are."

"I'm so happy for you both." Anne hugged her friend while Liam warmly shook Ron's hand in congratulations.

"We still have to tell our families, of course," Haley said, "but I know they're going to approve. My parents already like Ron very much and his family's going to love me, eventually. If I do a triple board and specialize in pediatric psychiatry, Ron and I might actually be able to work together in some ways."

She was off now, he thought, listening to her spinning plans with renewed enthusiasm. She'd be very busy during the few enforced weeks of her recuperation, planning a wedding and a full life afterward. Maybe he should be daunted by the lifelong commitment he'd just made, but for some reason he wasn't. The only thing that mattered to him was that he would always have Haley in his life. On his side. Just as he would always be there for her.

He had no doubt they could make it work. Her love had given him a new confidence in himself. He would be a better doctor, and a better man, because of it. Becoming convinced for the first time in his life that he had a great deal to offer in return, he looked ahead with a newfound optimism. He had finally discovered everything he'd ever wanted in his life—and this time, he wouldn't be walking away.

* * * * *

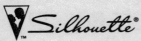
Silhouette®

COMING NEXT MONTH

Available July 27, 2010

SPECIAL EDITION

REQUEST YOUR FREE BOOKS!

2 FREE NOVELS PLUS 2 FREE GIFTS!

SPECIAL EDITION

Life, Love and Family!

YES! Please send me 2 FREE Silhouette® Special Edition® novels and my 2 FREE gifts (gifts are worth about $10). After receiving them, if I don't wish to receive any more books, I can return the shipping statement marked "cancel." If I don't cancel, I will receive 6 brand-new novels every month and be billed just $4.24 per book in the U.S. or $4.99 per book in Canada. That's a saving of 15% off the cover price! It's quite a bargain! Shipping and handling is just 50¢ per book.* I understand that accepting the 2 free books and gifts places me under no obligation to buy anything. I can always return a shipment and cancel at any time. Even if I never buy another book from Silhouette, the two free books and gifts are mine to keep forever.

235/335 SDN E5RG

Name	(PLEASE PRINT)

Address	Apt. #

City	State/Prov.	Zip/Postal Code

Signature (if under 18, a parent or guardian must sign)

Mail to the Silhouette Reader Service:
IN U.S.A.: P.O. Box 1867, Buffalo, NY 14240-1867
IN CANADA: P.O. Box 609, Fort Erie, Ontario L2A 5X3

Not valid for current subscribers to Silhouette Special Edition books.

Want to try two free books from another line?
Call 1-800-873-8635 or visit www.morefreebooks.com.

* Terms and prices subject to change without notice. Prices do not include applicable taxes. N.Y. residents add applicable sales tax. Canadian residents will be charged applicable provincial taxes and GST. Offer not valid in Quebec. This offer is limited to one order per household. All orders subject to approval. Credit or debit balances in a customer's account(s) may be offset by any other outstanding balance owed by or to the customer. Please allow 4 to 6 weeks for delivery. Offer available while quantities last.

Your Privacy: Silhouette is committed to protecting your privacy. Our Privacy Policy is available online at www.eHarlequin.com or upon request from the Reader Service. From time to time we make our lists of customers available to reputable third parties who may have a product or service of interest to you. If you would prefer we not share your name and address, please check here. ☐

Help us get it right—We strive for accurate, respectful and relevant communications. To clarify or modify your communication preferences, visit us at www.ReaderService.com/consumerchoice.

SSEI0R

HARLEQUIN®

A *Romance*

FOR EVERY MOOD™

Spotlight on
Heart & Home

Heartwarming romances
where love can happen
right when you least expect it.

See the next page to enjoy a sneak peek
from Harlequin® American Romance®,
a Heart and Home series.

"I hear you work miracles," Nate Hutchinson drawled.
Brooke Mitchell had just stepped into his lavishly appointed
office in downtown Fort Worth, Texas.

"Sometimes, I do." Brooke smiled and took the sexy
financier's hand in hers, shook it briefly.

"Good." Nate looked her straight in the eye. "Because
I'm in need of a home makeover—fast. The son of an old
friend is coming to live with me."

She was still tingling from the feel of his warm palm.
"Temporarily or permanently?"

"If all goes according to plan, I'll adopt Landry by
summer's end."

Brooke had heard the founder of Nate Hutchinson
Financial Services was eligible, wealthy and generous to a
fault. She hadn't known he was in the market for a family,
but she supposed she shouldn't be surprised. But Brooke
had figured a man as successful and handsome as Nate
would want one the old-fashioned way. *Not that this was
any of her business...*

"So what's the child like?" she asked crisply, trying not
to think how the marine-blue of Nate's dress shirt deepened
the hue of his eyes.

"I don't know." Nate took a seat behind his massive
antique mahogany desk. He relaxed against the smooth
leather of the chair. "I've never met him."

"Yet you've invited this kid to live with you permanently?"

"It's complicated. But I'm sure it's going to be fine."

Obviously Nate Hutchinson knew as little about teenage

boys as he did about decorating. But that wasn't her problem. Finding a way to do the assignment without getting the least bit emotionally involved was.

Find out how a young boy brings Nate and Brooke together in THE MOMMY PROPOSAL, coming August 2010 from Harlequin American Romance.

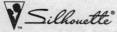

ROMANTIC

S U S P E N S E

Sparked by Danger, Fueled by Passion.

SILHOUETTE ROMANTIC SUSPENSE BRINGS YOU
AN ALL-NEW COLTONS OF MONTANA STORY!

FBI agent Jake Pierson is determined to solve his case,
even if it means courting and using the daughter of a
murdered informant. Mary Walsh hates liars and,
now that Jake has fallen deeply in love, he is afraid
to tell her the truth. But the truth is not the only
thing out there to hurt Mary…

Be part of the romance and suspense in

Covert Agent's Virgin Affair

by

LINDA CONRAD

Available August 2010 where books are sold.

Visit Silhouette Books at www.eHarlequin.com

HARLEQUIN *Presents*

The *Balfour Brides*

A powerful dynasty, eight daughters in disgrace...

Absolute scandal has rocked the core of the infamous Balfour family. The glittering, gorgeous daughters are in disgrace.... Banished from the Balfour mansion, they're sent to the boldest, most magnificent men to be wedded, bedded...and tamed!

And so begins a scandalous saga of dazzling glamour and passionate surrender.

Beginning August 2010

MIA AND THE POWERFUL GREEK—*Michelle Reid*
KAT AND THE DAREDEVIL SPANIARD—*Sharon Kendrick*
EMILY AND THE NOTORIOUS PRINCE—*India Grey*
SOPHIE AND THE SCORCHING SICILIAN—*Kim Lawrence*
ZOE AND THE TORMENTED TYCOON—*Kate Hewitt*
ANNIE AND THE RED-HOT ITALIAN—*Carol Mortimer*
BELLA AND THE MERCILESS SHEIKH—*Sarah Morgan*
OLIVIA AND THE BILLIONAIRE CATTLE KING—*Margaret Way*

8 volumes to collect and treasure!

---

www.eHarlequin.com

HP12934